W9-BMQ-295

FIXED
STARS

FIXED STARS

Marcie Gallacher

Bookcraft
Salt Lake City, Utah

All characters in this book are fictitious,
and any resemblance to actual persons,
living or dead, is purely coincidental.

Library of Congress Catalog Card Number: 99-71855

ISBN 1-57008-657-5

First Printing, 1999

Printed in the United States of America

To my children,
Jamie, Matthew, Brett,
and Michelle, with love!

Acknowledgments

Special thanks to my husband, Gray, and to my parents, Tal and LaRae Huber, for their constant love and support. I deeply appreciate the insightful staff at Bookcraft for making the publication of this book possible. Finally, loads of gratitude to Sandy Braniff, Kerri Freeman, Pat Barton, and Patty Johnson for supplying invaluable encouragement, comments, and criticism.

Grateful acknowledgment is given for permission to use the following material:

"The Blue Black Bug," a tongue twister by Mark Freeman of Orem, Utah.

"WORDS" FROM ARIEL by SYLVIA PLATH Copyright © 1966 by Ted Hughes. Copyright Renewed. Permission granted by HarperCollins Publishers, Inc.

We Shall Be Free
By Stephanie Davis and Garth Brooks
© 1992 EMI BLACKWOOD MUSIC INC., BEARTOOTH MUSIC, MAJOR BOB MUSIC and NO FENCES MUSIC
All Rights for BEARTOOTH MUSIC Controlled and Administered by EMI APRIL MUSIC INC.
All Rights Reserved International Copyright Secured Used by Permission

I want to know how God created this world. I am not interested in this or that phenomenon. I want to know His thoughts, the rest are details.

—Albert Einstein

The heavens, they are many, and they cannot be numbered unto man; but they are numbered unto me, for they are mine. . . .

For behold, this is my work and my glory—to bring to pass the immortality and eternal life of man.

—Moses 1:37, 39

Chapter 1

TRUTH OR DARE

"Truth," Andre said.

Katie, my six-year-old sister, coyly grinned up at him. "Andre, do you have a girlfriend?"

"Nope. My turn." Andre stretched, reaching for the flashlight. Katie jerked it away, the light beams streaming shadows across the dark tent walls.

She exploded into giggles. "You lied! Tracy's a girl, and she's your friend! So, she's your girlfriend!"

I moaned and wished I were an only child. An instant later Rob, my thirteen-year-old brother, pinned Katie and stripped the flashlight from her. Katie shrieked.

I sat cross-legged on my sleeping bag and shoved my hands into my jeans pockets. A few minutes before, Rob had dared me to eat an Oreo while chewing gum. I sighed and shrugged. It could have been worse. If I had chosen *truth* Rob might have asked me how I really felt about Andre.

My watch beeped. I pushed the glow button so that I could see the time. Nine-thirty. "Night, night, Kates. Robbie will tell you a ghost story!" I grabbed Andre's arm, and we ducked out of the tent before my brother and sister had time to protest. Earlier in the game I had dared Rob to stay in the tent until Katie fell asleep. He had to pay up.

I sank into a lawn chair and ignored the noises coming

from my siblings. The campfire had burned down to a low, glowing flame. I shivered and rubbed my bare arms. "I'm cold," I said as I smiled at Andre, "but there's no way I'm going in the tent to get my sweatshirt until Katie's asleep."

Andre grinned and threw a log on the fire. "I'll get you a blanket." He headed for his family's mobile home.

I thought about how I would have been on edge if I were alone with any other guy. But Andre and I had been close ever since I moved to California over two years earlier. My grandpa introduced us, and I got a job taking care of the horses at Andre's stepdad's estate. Andre and I had been through a lot together. But we were only friends; I had learned to accept that fact.

Our parents, Andre's mom and stepdad and my mom and dad, were taking a nighttime stroll along the beach. Earlier in the evening, after s'mores, Andre's mom, Anita, had turned to my mom and said, "The ocean is beautiful under a full moon. Let's take a romantic stroll with our hubbies."

I had smiled to myself because it sounded like the kind of stuff my dad would say when trying to get Mom in a romantic mood. But if Dad had said it, it would have sounded corny. In Anita's soft Brazilian accent, it just sounded great.

I had watched the adults walk away—Mom chattering about the colors of the waves and how she was going to set her easel up in the morning. (Mom was taking a beginning oil painting class.) Dad gave her his scientific opinion on where and when she should set up in order to get the best angle and light. (Dad thought he knew, due to his experience of teaching physics at the high school.)

In contrast, Anita and Grant, Andre's mom and stepdad, didn't say a word, but they held hands and walked close together. They'd only been married two years and were still in love. When I get married, I hope it's like that.

Andre put his lawn chair next to mine and draped a big wool blanket around us both. It was cozy and peaceful staring at the fire. You know you're really good friends with someone when you don't *have* to talk. Then Andre broke the silence. "Tracy, I'm going to miss Bart."

"Me too," I said quietly. Bart, my grandpa, was like a second father to Andre. A month before, Grandpa was diagnosed with cancer in advanced stages. It surprised all of us. Grandpa had a bad heart, but we never thought he would die of cancer.

I stared at the canopy of stars, thinking about what Grandpa had told me a long time ago. Searching the stars and thinking about the temple helped him deal with Grandma's death.

Andre stretched in front of the fire and crossed his ankles. His arms and legs had grown bigger and longer over the past year. He was taller than me, and his voice had become deeper. In the past his hair had been longer, with dark bangs in his eyes and a little curl at the nape of his neck. Now he kept it short. He stood up and walked halfway around the campfire. He squatted down and poked the fire with a stick. "Truth or dare?" he asked as he stared at the flames.

"What? I thought the game was over."

"Come on." He looked up at me through the flames. "Which is it?"

"Truth," I said.

"Tell me the truth!" Andre's brown eyes were luminous as the firelight danced around them. "How do you know that God is real? The Joseph Smith story and the Book of Mormon—they just sound so far-fetched. You know, stuff people make up so they can deal with life."

Now it was my turn to look into the fire. I felt Andre's eyes on me as I stared at the twisting flames. My stomach tightened.

Andre was very smart, and it was hard talking to him about the Church. Plus, it was not like he was illiterate when it came to Mormonism. He'd already had the missionary lessons. He had taken them after his mom joined the Church eighteen months before. Even then Andre took everything the elders said and analyzed it, questioned it—just as he did in Honors English when we discussed characters and themes. Ms. Hahn, our English teacher, loved how he could pick apart a book, but the missionaries weren't crazy about how he could pick apart a testimony. Neither was I. "Do you really want to know?" I looked straight into his eyes.

"Yeah, Trace." He shrugged his shoulders and came over and sat back down beside me. "Mom and Bart and Kallie—they always tell me how they feel about the Church." (I noticed that Andre said "the" Church instead of "your" Church. That seemed encouraging.) He went on, "But, when it comes to serious religious discussions, *you* tend to clam up."

"OK." I sucked in a deep breath and plunged in. "It's just a feeling I have, when I pray. It's kind of like peace and excitement. And everything makes sense, and you feel like Heavenly Father is whispering to you that it's true. It's like a burning inside, and you know your prayers are answered."

"Through the Holy Ghost?"

"Yeah. Through the Holy Ghost."

"That's what my mom and Bart say."

"When Kallie read the Joseph Smith story," I added hopefully, "she felt like she was hearing something she had always known. Like déjà vu." Andre nodded thoughtfully.

For a moment, I thought about Kallie. She was our other best friend. We made an interesting trio—a guy from Brazil, a blond from Michigan, and a tall, pretty African-American. Actually, Kallie was only half black. Her dad was white. Her parents had divorced a long time before, and Kallie saw her dad for only a couple of weeks each summer. That's why she wasn't with us—she was visiting her dad.

Kallie wanted to join the Church, but she couldn't. Her mom wanted her to wait until she was twenty-one. On the other hand, Andre's mom would have been overjoyed if he had joined the Church. But of course he hadn't. He didn't believe in it.

Andre spoke quietly. "I try to pray sometimes, but it never works for me. I prayed when my dad was shot. But he kept bleeding."

Andre's dad was shot on a bus in Brazil. Andre watched him die. Would I believe in Heavenly Father if that had happened to me?

"I prayed that Grandpa would get better," I said quietly, "but he's not going to this time. He's going to die."

"But, Tracy, you still believe in God?"

"Yeah," I said, "I still do."

Andre shrugged. "I just don't get it."

Andre didn't get it! I thought about all of the things I didn't get. I remembered earlier that summer when Kallie, Andre, and I spent a week on a school-sponsored trip to Washington, D.C. During a tour of French impressionist paintings at the National Gallery of Art, Ms. Hahn started sniffling and wiping her eyes.

"Look at Renoir's people," she choked. "They invite you to know them and love them. But Cézanne! His people in this painting push you away like they're afraid you might hurt them." She started crying harder. We all stared at Ms. Hahn. All of us except Kallie. Kallie's warm brown eyes filled with empathetic tears, and she hugged Ms. Hahn.

I didn't get it. I thought the paintings were neat, but I didn't *feel* them like Ms. Hahn and Kallie. Why would those paintings make them cry?

There was another thing that I didn't get. When we got back from D.C., Andre and I gave Grant, a Vietnam veteran, a rubbing he wanted of a buddy's name on the Vietnam Veterans Memorial.

A few days later, I was over at their house when Grant was mounting the rubbing on black matte board. The strange thing was that it was slightly torn and there were wrinkle marks all through it, like the paper had been mangled and smoothed out again. I asked Grant if someone had accidentally thrown it away. No, Grant had said, it hadn't been an accident. I didn't get it. Did Grant almost destroy something he treasured? I didn't understand Vietnam. Maybe there are some things you have to experience to understand.

"Andre." I turned away from the fire and looked at him. "Truth or dare?"

"Dare."

"I was hoping you'd pick that."

"Why?"

"Because I have a dare for you. I dare you to read the Book of Mormon. All of it. Then pray about it. Maybe then you'll understand."

Andre looked at me. He smiled. "Trace," he said, "maybe I'll take your dare."

Chapter 2

PARALLEL UNIVERSES

Two weeks passed and school started. On Thursday afternoon, I finished my homework and drove our decrepit little Honda out to the Montagues' to exercise and groom the horses.

After I pulled into the big circular driveway, I found Andre, Grant, and two men who were strangers to me carrying boxes from an oversized pickup into the Montagues' guest house. Perplexed, I wondered who the men were. The Montagues had plenty of money. They didn't need to bother with renters.

I turned off the engine and slowly climbed out of the car. I gazed at the guest house, remembering how Andre's family used to live there when he was a little kid. It was a quaint cottage standing about two hundred yards from the Montagues' stately, colonial-style home. Years ago, it was the servants' quarters. Back then Andre's parents were second-class citizens—Grant's hired help. But that was history. Now Andre's dad was dead, and Grant was married to his mom.

"Hey, Trace." Andre waved and motioned me over. As I approached, I looked more carefully at the strangers. One was a middle-aged black man about medium height with a salt-and-pepper moustache, dark skin, and deep wrinkle lines around his eyes. His graying hair matched the color of his worn summer suit.

The other was young, over six feet, slender, and muscled. He was black too but lighter complexioned, hardly any darker than Kallie. His skin had golden undertones as if he'd been out in the sun. He slouched slightly in a long mustard T-shirt. I looked at his baggy black pants, his Nikes, his shaven head, the earring in his left ear, and his zits.

"Tracy." Grant strolled up to me and put his arm around my shoulder. "Meet some friends of mine. This is the Reverend Theo Smith and his son, Marcus. They drove up from Los Angeles today. Theo's flying back home tomorrow, but Marcus is staying. He's a senior like you and Andre. I'm trusting you two to show Marcus the ropes at school." Grant's metallic blue-gray eyes smiled into mine, and I knew he was asking a favor. Then, turning to the Reverend Smith and his son, he added, "Tracy's like part of the family. She helps us with the horses. We couldn't do without her."

I grinned at Grant as thoughts of Kallie distracted me. That happens sometimes. Thoughts of people I care about crowd my mind like sudden winds on a calm day. Up until this moment, Kallie had been the only African-American in our graduating class. Now there was Marcus. I thought of the people who wanted to hang around Kallie just because of her color and of the other people who stayed away from her for the same reason. Kallie joked about it. It didn't seem to bother her, and she was always nice to everyone. Yet I wondered how she felt deep inside. I wondered how Marcus would like northern California and Haltsburg High.

I pushed my long, wavy darkish blond hair out of my face. Then I turned to Marcus, smiled, and said, "Hi."

Marcus nodded slightly. His stony gaze met mine. I looked down uncomfortably. His eyes were dark and cold, masklike, so different from Kallie's brown eyes, which were warm and constant as the sun. Then there were Andre's eyes, constantly changing—burning with questions one minute, then smiling the next. I looked back at Marcus. His eyes pushed me away. Hard.

Then the Reverend Smith took my hand. "Tracy, it *is* a pleasure meeting you. God bless you." I turned to him. He had a huge smile, so warm and kind that it thawed the chill left by his son.

"It's nice meeting you too," I said. Then my thoughts became a flood of questions. First of all, I'd practically lived at the Montagues' for two years, but I'd never heard a whisper of Theo or Marcus Smith. Second, Grant Montague was a high-powered businessman. He wasn't religious, although he used to be a Mormon back before Vietnam. Somehow, this soft-spoken minister didn't fit in with any of Grant's friends or acquaintances. Third, and weirdest of all, was Andre's silence. Why hadn't he told me about Marcus?

Andre brought me back to reality by bumping his knee into the back of mine. I lurched forward, then grabbed his arm and punched him.

"Andre." Grant interrupted our exchange. "Why don't you, Marcus, and Tracy go riding. Theo and I can manage this stuff."

"Great!" Andre grinned.

"I'll stay and unpack," Marcus said shortly. He picked up another box and carried it into the guest house. He obviously didn't want anything to do with us.

Andre and I walked to the barn. "We don't talk for a day, and the world changes," I whispered.

"It's a long story," Andre said under his breath. We grabbed leads and went out into the pasture to find Paulo and Gozo. While we walked, Andre began to explain. Theo Smith was a minister in Los Angeles. He and Grant had been buddies in Vietnam. Two nights before, Theo had called. Marcus had been attacked by a gang of white supremacist guys. Theo needed to get Marcus away. He asked if Marcus could come stay with Grant for a while.

"Grant said yes." Andre shrugged. "He told us he owed Theo big time."

"Did Theo save his life or something?" I asked.

"He didn't say."

We walked in silence. I thought of news clips I'd seen of gang violence in L.A., the Ku Klux Klan, and burning churches. Haltsburg was a small, mostly white town. We didn't have problems like that.

"I don't think Marcus wants to be here," Andre commented. "He'd prefer another universe."

"Maybe he'll warm up," I suggested.

Andre shrugged again.

"Speaking of other universes," I said, changing the subject, "tell me about worm holes."

Andre was a science fiction buff and had recently been reading a book about hyperspace. The last time we had talked, he told me a theory about parallel universes that were connected by structures called *worm holes.*

"They're smaller than microscopic, infinitesimally small." Andre grinned. He loved big words. Then he added, "But scientists are almost positive they exist."

"How can they know that?" I asked skeptically.

"Through computers and math and the laws of physics. You know."

"Sure, like I really know." I laughed shortly and added, "You plug a few equations into the computer and bingo, you prove there are other universes. Presto, now there are worm holes connecting them."

"It's all in knowing the right equations," Andre said. Then he tripped me. On purpose. I grabbed hold of his arm to keep my balance. I liked the way his arm felt on my hand. It wasn't super buff, like Marcus's, but it was firm and warm. Andre tried to trip me again.

"Quit it!" I dropped his arm and punched him.

A few minutes later, we found Paulo grazing nonchalantly. Gozo, on the other hand, was trying to figure out how to get past an electric wire. We walked them back to the barn and saddled up. Paulo was Andre's horse. He was black and huge. Gozo was a flighty Arabian two-year-old. His coat was a pretty strawberry roan color. He still needed a lot of training, but I'd loved him ever since he was a baby.

We were trotting the horses down the road when Andre started talking about the book again.

"Scientists think there are up to ten dimensions in the universe. Trace, we can't see them because the human brain can perceive only three dimensions."

"You mean there might be other dimensions all around us, but we don't know it just 'cause we're human? That's very weird."

"Actually, it's pretty cool. The laws of nature become simpler and more perfect if you plug in more dimensions."

Gozo shied for no reason at all. I sat deep in the saddle to keep my balance. Then I circled him until he settled.

"Since Gozo's not human maybe he can perceive the other dimensions," I said. "Maybe that's why he's so wacky!" Andre laughed as I urged Gozo into a lope. I decided to give Gozo a workout. Maybe that would calm him down. I could hear Andre behind me on Paulo.

I slowed down when I neared Grandpa's land. He still owned five acres even though he didn't live there anymore. It had become an area of mostly weeds and a burned-out foundation. But two years before it was the greatest place in the world—a renovated one-room schoolhouse which Grandpa lived in, with tons of gorgeous landscaping.

Back then Andre came over every day to help Grandpa keep up the property. That's how they became so close. Andre's dad was gone, and they needed each other. Then Grandpa had a heart attack, and there was a fire. I'd never forget that day. Grandpa wasn't home when the schoolhouse burned, but I saw the fire. I ran into the flames, trying to rescue something that was important to Grandpa. It left me with an ugly scar on my left arm.

After the fire Grandpa moved to an apartment in town. I shuddered. Pretty soon Grandpa, like his once beautiful home, would be gone. Gozo tensed up. Maybe he could feel my mood. I took a deep breath and patted his shoulder. "Relax, Buddy."

"Tracy," Andre broke into my thoughts, "This book talks about other things too. It talks about God. The author says that most scientists believe in a kind of Cosmic Order in the universe. But that's different from the God of miracles that religions preach about. Religion can make rational people totally irrational, and it causes some of man's inhumanity towards other men, like in holy wars. The book also says that we are children of the stars. The atoms in our bodies were forged trillions of years ago when a star exploded. We're made of star dust."

I liked the "made of star dust" stuff, but I didn't like the things Andre was saying about God. I believed in a God of miracles, and Andre knew it.

Andre went on. "This author sounds like a really strong person. He doesn't need a God of miracles to give his life meaning. He thinks there is meaning enough in his life."

I'm not irrational or weak because I believe in God, I thought. I'm stronger and better because I believe in God.

I turned towards Andre. "God's real. It was faith in Him that helped me through *that*." I pointed to the burned-out foundation. Andre knew I was talking about the fire and everything that happened afterwards. "And faith in God will help me through Grandpa's death," I added.

I must have sounded defensive, because Andre said, "Tracy, I'm not putting you down because you believe in God."

"I know," I said, and I forced myself to smile. But I ached

inside. I wished more than anything that Andre believed in God, that he felt the same way I did. But I didn't know what else to say.

"Casey's going to call tonight, so I had better start back," I said. Casey was my older sister, who was a sophomore at Brigham Young University.

Andre and I turned Paulo and Gozo around. When we got back to the barn, we groomed the horses outside and talked about other things—homework, teachers, and people at school. We were almost finished when I looked toward the guest house and saw Marcus staring at us through one of the windows. The rays of the setting sun hit his high cheekbones, making the rest of his face look dark and angular. He saw me watching him, and he didn't look away.

I touched Andre's arm and motioned towards the guest house window with my eyes. Andre looked up. When he saw Marcus, he grinned, waved, and yelled for him to come outside with us. Marcus shook his head and turned away from the window.

I looked at Andre. He was trying so hard to help Marcus feel at home. I gently punched him in the shoulder. "You're just about the nicest guy in the world," I said.

"I'm not perfect," Andre said.

"Really?"

"Yeah. I'm not a member of your church."

"You're right," I said, teasing. "You're not perfect." But inside, I felt like a shadow had passed between us. Andre finished up with the horses while I went into the barn to clean the bridles.

When I came out, Andre was taking Paulo to the paddock. "Thanks for helping," I called as I headed toward my car.

"Anytime." Andre flipped his hand up in a wave. "See ya tomorrow, Trace."

I started the car. Unexpectedly, I was flooded with a

sense of relief. I was glad to be getting away from the dark stranger whom Andre would have to learn to live with. I was glad to be going home to my family—my normal, ordinary family, who laughed, argued, and worked together.

Right then, I realized that there was something very special about my family. To us, God was like an axiom on which the rest of the universe was based, while to Andre God was a theorem you constantly tried to prove or disprove. I sighed, glad to be going home to my family, my universe.

Chapter 3

THE PATHWAY TO TRUTH

I kicked our bursting locker hard in an attempt to shut it. I kicked it again. "Our locker should be in *The Guinness Book of World Records* for sloppiness," I said moodily. Kallie studied me with her backpack resting on her hip. Her light denim overalls softened the sharp angles of Kallie's arms and legs. Her long black hair hung in a hundred slender braids held together at the bottom with a rubber band.

"Easy does it, girl. That's my locker too. What's eating you?"

I gazed at Kallie.

"ADD again?" Kallie asked. I couldn't help smiling. Kallie knew me pretty well. She would say that I suffered from ADD—Andre Deficit Disorder. All during the previous year she advised me to date other people, expand my horizons, keep Andre as a friend. It was not as easy as it sounded. Maybe it would have been different *if* I'd had great guys flocking around me, or *if* I'd had more confidence. Still, my relationship with Andre wasn't the thing eating me that day. It was Grandpa.

I told Kallie about Grandpa moving in with us. Mom got him a walker and a wheelchair. Then she began researching hospital beds and hospice care. I hated it.

"I'm sorry, Trace. Man, I'm really sorry." Kallie squeezed my hand. Then Brice Miller sauntered up.

"Kallie Thompson! And Emerald Eyes!" Brice strung his arm around my waist. I wiggled out of his grasp. Technically, Brice was a Mormon, but you'd have never known it by his looks. He was a throwback from the sixties, a nature boy who dyed his hair a different color each month. At that moment, it was lemon yellow.

Brice should have graduated the spring before, but he spent his senior year hanging around the drag strip and playing the guitar. The principal gave him a fifth year to get his act together. Supposedly, Brice was going to get his diploma that December and go on a mission the following spring. I'd believe it when I saw it.

"Hey, Brice," I said, not very enthusiastically. Rumor had it that Brice liked me. I wanted to discourage that. A gust of wind whipped my hair into my mouth. I dug a scrunchy out of my pocket and wound my hair into it.

"Oh, man," Brice interjected, raising his pale eyebrows at me. "Doesn't hair just drive you crazy when it's down! It does me. Especially yours."

"Be quiet, Brice," I smiled at him. A patient, irritated, maternal kind of smile.

"Come on, Bricey, walk me to class." Kallie grabbed Brice's arm. Kallie was a true friend.

I picked up my books and took off to find Andre. We had first period together—AP English.

Fifteen minutes later, we were sitting in class. It was our weekly poetry interpretation day. Ms. Hahn read aloud the poem on our handout:

> The wayfarer,

Perceiving the pathway to truth,
Was struck with astonishment.
It was thickly grown with weeds.
"Ha," he said,
"I see that no one has passed here
In a long time."
Later he saw that each weed
Was a singular knife.
"Well," he mumbled at last,
"Doubtless there are other roads."

"OK, people," Ms. Hahn said, pacing. "Stephen Crane died when he was twenty-nine years old." (Ms. Hahn had this bizarre habit of telling us how old an author was at the time of his demise.) She continued, "What did he mean when he said that the pathway to truth was thickly grown with weeds?"

Silence pooled through the class. "Any volunteers, or should I call on someone?" Ms. Hahn's short black hair screamed around her face. She stalked through the room, staring at each of us, like a cat in search of her prey.

Andre raised his hand. Ms. Hahn grinned and pointed a long finger at him.

"The weeds indicate that not many people have gone that way. They don't have the courage to seek the truth."

"Good. Why don't they have enough courage?"

"Because each blade of grass is a knife which could cut them," Andre said. "In other words, the truth hurts."

Ms. Hahn laughed delightedly. "People, let's talk about this. Do you agree or disagree? What are these truths that are like knives? What other paths do people choose so that they can avoid the pathway to truth?"

Toni Harris's hand shot up. Toni was petite with billowing red hair. She acted as if she were thirty, not seventeen. Her goals in life were to get the English Award and a "5" on the AP exam. "Drugs and alcohol," Toni smiled primly.

"Sometimes people get high when reality is too painful, when truth hurts."

"Very perceptive, Toni. Anybody else?" Ms. Hahn asked.

"Maybe the painful truths are things like death and disease," I offered, "things that are hard to face." I thought about Mom, her perpetual optimism, how she didn't like to discuss poverty, drugs, or Grandpa's illness. I felt everyone staring at me, and I realized that I had forgotten to raise my hand. My cheeks felt hot.

"Excellent comment," Ms. Hahn said. "Facing our own mortality can be excruciating. What other paths do people take to avoid the truth? Andre, any thoughts?"

Andre shuffled his feet under his chair. "What about religion? That's another path. People can pretend that death isn't the end. They get defensive when science punches holes in their beliefs. Think, for example, of the anger toward Galileo, and toward the theory of evolution."

I looked down at my hands. Great, I thought. Andre's supposed to be reading the Book of Mormon with an open mind. But he sees religion as another path running perpendicular to truth. If he hadn't been so smart and good, if I hadn't cared about him, then maybe I could have discounted everything he said. I suddenly wished that Kallie had chosen to take AP English, that she were beside me lending moral support.

"Thought provoking!" Ms. Hahn smiled at Andre. She thought Andre was someone really special.

Toni Harris cut in. "Example," she said expertly. "Take the controversy about R-rated movies in the school—how religious groups in town want them totally banned. It doesn't matter whether what happens in the movie is true. These religious people are so closed minded. They can't handle the truth."

My heart pounded in my chest. I was one of those "religious" people. It was my bishop who had mobilized the town in an effort to ban R-rated movies in the school.

Just the past week, there had been an article about the controversy in the *Haltsburg Herald.* The piece contained a quote from Ms. Hahn about the dangers of censorship and the need to disregard ratings and choose excellence. But the paper had also printed a quote from Bishop Leriway about the right and responsibility of parents to protect minors from violence and pornography. The article closed with these words, "The school board will listen to both sides at their next meeting—so Haltsburg will have fireworks this fall!"

To complicate things, the whole controversy was hard on my dad. He was one of Bishop Leriway's counselors and also a teacher at the high school with a principal and close friends who had strong feelings about the rights of educators.

After class, Ms. Hahn came up to Andre and me. "Excellent comments in class today." She addressed us both. Then she turned to Andre. "Tryouts for *The Winter's Tale* are Monday. Be ready. Mr. Rice makes the final cuts." Andre nodded and gave her a thumbs up.

"Tracy," Ms. Hahn said thoughtfully to me. "Have you thought about getting involved in the play? The female parts aren't set in stone."

"I've got mega stage fright," I answered.

"There's plenty to do behind the scenes," Ms. Hahn added. "Costumes, lighting, staging."

"I'll think about it." I grinned. Both Kallie and Andre were in the drama club and were hoping for leading roles. But I was too self-conscious. What would it be like to shed inhibitions and shine?

"Your dad told me your grandfather has moved in with you." Ms. Hahn laid her long fingers on my arm. "I was thinking about your family last night. I copied a poem for you."

She took an envelope off her desk and handed it to me. It was very nice of her to be so concerned. The next class began trickling in, so I didn't have time to read it right then. I folded it up and slid it into my pocket.

"You two stay out of trouble." Ms. Hahn smiled crookedly at us as we left.

As Andre and I walked towards my locker, I pulled the poem out of my pocket and read it aloud.

> That time of year thou mayst in me behold
> When yellow leaves, or none, or few, do hang
> Upon those boughs which shake against the cold,
> Bare ruined choirs, where late the sweet birds sang.
> In me thou seest the twilight of such day
> As after sunset fadeth in the west,
> Which by and by black night doth take away,
> Death's second self that seals up all in rest . . .
> This thou perceiv'st, which makes thy love more strong,
> To love that well which thou must leave ere long.

I thought about Grandpa dying and about how Ms. Hahn cared about me enough to give me the poem. I thought about what Sister Miller, Brice's mom, had said the Sunday before—that any teacher in favor of R-rated movies was on Satan's side. I felt alone and confused. Tears jumped to my eyes. Andre must have noticed, because he put his arm around me.

"It's a good poem," he said. "Who's it by?"

"Shakespeare," I said as I brushed a tear away with my sleeve and made myself smile. "Ms. Hahn forgot to write down how old he was when he died," I joked lamely.

"Fifty-two," Andre filled in the blank. "I've known Hahn for a long time." This struck me as strangely funny, and I giggled. Then we were both laughing, and Andre pulled me closer. I didn't move away.

Chapter 4

Nailing Jello to a Tree

On Friday night, Andre and Kallie came over to read *The Winter's Tale* aloud with me. The idea was to practice for Monday's tryouts. Andre was hoping to get the part of Leontes, and Kallie wanted to be Hermione, his wife. I teasingly offered to buy them a wedding gift.

Kallie ignored my comment and talked Rob and Grandpa into reading with us, since we needed more male voices. The reading was fun, even though Rob tripped over his lines and totally overacted. Kallie and I laughed at Andre, who kept trying to educate everybody by explaining the old English expressions. All the while, Grandpa lent constant encouragement by listening intently to each reader, chuckling sometimes, and occasionally clapping his hands and exclaiming "Bravo!" when the acting was good. Angel, my lame Doberman, snored through it all.

During the final scene, I watched as Kallie and Andre exchanged lines. By that time Kallie had settled into her part, and they both were incredible actors. I glanced at Grandpa. His eyes shone as he listened. Even Robbie was uncharacteristically quiet. Could he actually be spellbound by the beauty of the language? I felt an aching kind of happiness—as if my life were a play and this scene would be over too soon.

Then it ended. We said our good nights to Grandpa, and Andre and I walked Kallie out to her car. She had to go home to baby-sit for her sister, Danika. Two years before, Danika was a senior. She was one of the first people I met as a new sophomore at Haltsburg High. As head cheerleader, she was popular, friendly, and outspoken. Now she was divorced, had a baby, and worked night shifts at Malloy's Restaurant.

After Kallie left, Andre and I sat on the front porch step. Angel squeezed between us. She sniffed my pocket, and I pulled out the remains of a Snickers bar and gave it to her. Angel scarfed down the chocolate, then nestled her head in my lap. Andre stared into the night, deep in thought. I wondered if he was trying to figure out the unifying theory of the universe.

I looked down at Angel and stroked her forehead. My thoughts centered on simpler things. I remembered the March evening, less than a year before, when Andre and I found Angel. We were in his Toyota on our way home from the feed store. It was dusk. I had spotted a dog lying on the side of the road. Andre stopped, and I jumped out of the truck and ran to the animal. I knelt down and cried out when I saw her crushed front leg, her torn ear. I looked up at Andre standing beside me. There was anger in his eyes. He swore at the hit-and-run driver who left her there.

Then Andre had grabbed a blanket from the truck bed and helped me wrap the dog in it. She whined softly as he carried her. I climbed into the passenger seat, and he laid her on my lap. Her blood soaked through the blanket, through my jeans, and onto my bare leg. Andre drove the red Toyota truck as if it were an ambulance.

At the animal hospital, the vet sedated the dog and told us he could save her by amputating her leg and cauterizing the stub. The receptionist looked up the number on the dog's tag and called the owner. He said to put the dog out of her misery, that she was show stock and now worthless.

But Andre and I couldn't let her die. We told the vet that we would pay for the surgery. Andre called his mom, and she backed up our decision. After the operation, Anita had arrived, and she and Andre took the dog home. Together, Anita, Andre, and I nursed her back to health. She had the best temperament—patient, intelligent, and gentle. We found out that her registered name was "Watch over Me." We nicknamed her "Angel."

Three weeks later, on my birthday, Andre had brought Angel over with a card that pictured a bulldog licking a baby. Inside it read, "To my dog-gonest best friend. Happy Birthday."

Then he said that Angel was mine forever. Andre told me my parents had agreed. They had decided it wasn't such a bad idea—having an angel watch over their teenage daughter, especially if the angel was a Doberman. Also, Angel was having a hard time keeping up with Andre's dog, Potok.

I had hugged Andre and told him it was the best present ever. I couldn't believe that Angel was really mine. As part of our family, Angel hopped around the house on three legs with her crushed ear and sweet eyes, everyone's best friend.

Stroking Angel's mangled ear, I wondered once more what Andre was thinking about. Long, thin clouds crossed over the sliver of moon, reminding me of Ms. Hahn's fingers.

"Gozo did good today," I remarked, referring to our ride earlier in the day.

"Yeah," Andre said. "He's settling down. Think Bart will be around for *The Winter's Tale?*" When Andre said "around" we both knew he meant "alive."

"I hope so," I said. Now I knew what Andre was thinking about. He was thinking about Grandpa. The play was scheduled for December fourth. This was mid-October. When

Andre had played Hamlet as a freshman, Grandpa had helped him with his lines and cheered him on. Andre was remembering that.

"We're going up to the mountains tomorrow," I said. "Grandpa wants to see the fall colors." (I didn't say "for the last time.") "Want to come?" I offered.

"Sure. I was going to golf. Kevin's coming down, and Grant has a tee time at Dry Creek. But they can go without me." Kevin was Andre's stepbrother, Grant's son. He was a student at the University of California, Davis. He and my older sister, Casey, had a history. Kevin was *not* one of my favorite people.

"Does Marcus ever golf with you guys?" I asked.

"Does Marcus do anything with us?" Andre answered, cracking his knuckles. Andre was right. Marcus led a solitary life. He ate alone, slept alone, drove around in his truck—all alone. He pushed away the Montagues' efforts to make him feel at home, to be his friends.

Not even Kallie, with her brilliant smile, had been able to thaw Marcus's icy shell. I remembered the time I first pointed him out to her, six weeks before during Government class.

"That's one good-looking man," Kallie had whispered. Then she had started coming out to the Montagues' with me, showing a sudden interest in mucking out stalls. Almost every afternoon, Marcus would be there, his shirt wadded on the ground, his bare chest shiny in the heat as he washed and waxed his truck. He seemed determined not to let one particle of dust settle on it.

One day, Kallie tried to talk to him as he worked. "That's one cool truck. A classic."

"Thanks."

"I like the running boards and the big tires."

"Thanks."

"What's the year and make?"

"1970. Ford Custom."

"Is it yours?"

"Yep."

"Is that the original green paint?"

"Nope. I fixed it up last year."

"Want some help?" Kallie asked. Marcus threw her a rag and she started rubbing the truck's fender. "Do you like it here in Haltsburg?" she asked.

"Nope."

After that, Kallie helped Marcus almost every day, with a sweat band around her forehead, her hundred braids swinging back and forth as she shined his truck. But Marcus still didn't warm up. It bugged me—the way he practically ignored her, the way he acted as though her help meant nothing.

Once, when we were alone, I asked her about it. "Kal," I said, "why do you give him the time of day?"

Kallie explained: "Do you remember those paintings Ms. Hahn cried over at the National Gallery of Art? I can't remember the artist. But Ms. Hahn said that the people in the paintings looked like they were pushing you away because they were afraid you might hurt them. Marcus reminds me of that."

I thought about how Kallie volunteered her time at the Pediatric Urgent Care Center, how she was a student mediator and worked the Teen Crisis Line. Kallie wanted to change the world.

"Kal, you have PMS," I teased. "Poor Marcus Syndrome."

Kallie just laughed and kept trying. At school, she'd wave to Marcus and flash him smiles. She would pull me over, and we'd sit by him in Government. But it was futile. He hardly acknowledged our existence.

"Kal, you need to move on," I said, "to think about other men."

"There are no other men," Kallie said. Then she raised her eyebrows at me. "And, girl, you don't have room to talk." We both knew she was referring to Andre.

"It's hopeless," I said. "It's like nailing jello to a tree."

"Are you referring to my PMS or your ADD?" Kallie laughed as she flipped her many braids.

"Both," I said. Then we both cracked up. We laughed at our nonexistent love lives until we had tears in our eyes.

Chapter 5

THE YELLOW TIME

Next morning around the breakfast table, Mom made an announcement. "I talked to Casey today. She's getting serious about that Idaho farm boy, Chet Wagner."

"Mom, why do you call Casey at six on Saturday mornings? I'm asleep, and I don't get to talk to her," I complained between bites of scrambled egg.

"Your mom wants Casey to herself. She sneaks out of the bedroom without a sound." Dad looked at Mom over the rim of his glasses.

"Mom, don't you think Space Case would like to sleep in once a week?" Robbie asked.

"It's an hour later in Provo, and it's the only time I'm sure to catch her," Mom replied cheerfully. "Anyway, she wants to bring Chet home for Thanksgiving."

"An Idaho potatohead! No!" Robbie writhed as if he were in pain.

"Chet isn't a person's name, it's a hamster's name!" Katie piped in.

"What is Chet majoring in?" Dad was suddenly very interested.

"I don't know," Mom mused. "I wonder what his family is like."

"Come on!" I interrupted vehemently. "Case dates lots of

guys. It's not like they're engaged!" Everyone stared at me. I played with the egg on my fork. Why on earth did I feel so irritated?

An hour later, Andre was over, and our van was packed for the picnic in the mountains. Katie insisted on riding with Andre and me in the truck. As Angel was already curled up in the cab's small backseat, Katie ended up in the front, perched between us. On the way, she took charge of the radio, rifling it back and forth between Rock 97 and Country 103, singing the songs she knew at the top of her shrill little-girl voice.

After two hours of Katie's medley, I made a mental note to gag her on the way home. Finally, we arrived at a deserted campground. Immediately, Rob and Katie burst out of the two vehicles and checked out the nearby creek. Angel barked and hopped swiftly around, sniffing and wagging her tail joyfully. Dad set up the wheelchair, and Andre helped Grandpa out of the van.

The air felt cool and smelled tangy from the pines. Then, as Grandpa attempted to sit down in the wheelchair, he suddenly gripped Andre's hand. Grandpa's face turned pale from pain. Mom quickly opened a can of Seven Up and pulled some pills from her purse. She helped Grandpa take them.

After about ten minutes, Grandpa's color returned, and he was settled comfortably in his wheelchair. Andre gently rubbed his shoulders. Mom quickly set out lunch. We dined on tuna sandwiches, fruit salad, chips, and cookies. I noticed that Andre wasn't eating.

After lunch, Katie climbed carefully into Grandpa's lap. "Katie," Grandpa said as he stroked her blond curls, "remember when you were little and I took you fishing at Donner?"

"Grandpa, we went fishing lots of times," Katie said.

"Yes, but that time you named the fish—Starshine, Swimfast, the Hunchback of Donner Lake."

Katie giggled. "I don't remember. Was I three or four?"

"Who knows?" Grandpa chuckled. "But you told me you wanted to come back again during the 'yellow time.' And here we are, back in the mountains during the 'yellow time.' "

Grandpa's eyes were shining, and I suddenly remembered some of the words from Ms. Hahn's poem. I paraphrased them the best I could, because I knew Grandpa would like them. "That time of year which we behold when yellow leaves do shake against the cold. This, which makes our love more strong, to love that well which we must leave ere long."

Grandpa smiled a "thank you" at me. Dad wiped his eyes, and Robbie wolfed down a cookie. Andre sat still as stone.

"Picture time!" Mom jumped up with her camera. She deserves the Pollyanna award for cheerfulness.

Mom snapped pictures of each of us with Grandpa, then all of us together. She photographed Katie coaxing a squirrel to eat from her hand and Robbie tossing sticks to Angel.

After that, Andre and I skipped rocks in the creek. I stopped and looked up at the sky. There wasn't a cloud. The camera clicked, and I whirled around. "Mother, ask first!"

"I couldn't help it," Mom grinned. "You looked elegant and dreamy staring at the sky."

"You mean skinny and spacey," I returned.

Mom laughed. "No," she said, "I meant elegant and dreamy."

The wind picked up, and Andre tucked his hands into his jeans pockets.

Mom snapped Andre's picture. He smiled, but the smile didn't look real. "Andre, I hope you don't mind," Mom said.

"She couldn't help it. You looked so masculine and remote," I said and grinned at Andre.

"Tracy means handsome and hunkish!" Robbie yelled.

I felt my face get hot. "Let's go on a walk," I said. "Time to get away from the photographic maniac and the irritating adolescent!"

We took our shoes off and crossed the creek. The water was freezing. On the other side, I rubbed my feet to warm them before redoing my socks and shoes. Andre put his shoes back on quickly and efficiently.

We had hiked about twenty minutes when we came to a grove of aspen trees. The leaves were bright yellow and roundish—like discs of gold cut out from the surrounding evergreens. The sun skipped through. It was beautiful. "I love these trees," I exclaimed.

"Trace." Andre hardly seemed to notice the beauty of the grove. This wasn't like him. Andre and I both had a thing for trees. "Do you think we'll forget the things we did with your grandfather? Like Katie forgot the fishing trip? Sometimes I can't even picture my dad."

"We won't forget," I said. "Besides, Mom's taking pictures, and we're writing our memories down. Your dad died so suddenly." I looked again at the golden aspen leaves. "We'll all die someday," I added. "Then we'll see Grandpa again."

"No one knows if there really is life after death," Andre said, kicking a rock hard. "Face it, your mom hides behind her camera. You hide behind your religious beliefs. You guys can't handle the truth."

Suddenly, I felt an uncontrollable flash of anger at Andre. I took a deep breath, trying to control my emotions, trying to see things from his perspective. His dad had died, and now he was losing my grandpa. Didn't he understand that there was an ocean of hurt in me too? But you can't cry all the time. I had invited Andre up to the mountains to spend a wonderful day—a day that would never come again. Mom was remembering with her camera. My faith gave me hope. He had no right to say those things. He had no right to pull the carpet of my faith out from under me.

"What are you going to do," I snapped, "stay mad at the world? You told me you would read the Book of Mormon, but you haven't. You think I'm hiding behind my faith, but you don't know anything about it!"

"Maybe I don't understand your faith, but I know what I'm going to do." Andre's eyes flashed fire. "I'm going to find out as much as I can about the universe and the human body. I'm going to be part of the world of research, of science and medicine. I'm going to have power over disease and death. I'm not going to hide! I'm going to help people win!"

Andre glared at me as though he were daring the universe to challenge him. I looked right back into his eyes. "You might win some battles," I said, "but you'll lose the war. Everybody dies." I whirled around and started back towards my family.

Andre caught up with me. "Trace," he said, conciliatory now, "let's forget this. I'm sorry." Maybe his wave of anger had passed, but I was still caught in the wake.

"OK," I said shortly. We walked back together in silence. But even with the sun shining, I felt angry, cold, and afraid as the golden aspen leaves were crushed under my feet.

Chapter 6

PREJUDICE

On Monday, Andre met me at my locker after school. We had patched together our friendship, and I was excited about watching him and Kallie try out for the play. When we got to the auditorium, Kallie had saved seats for us near the back. I plopped down next to Kal, and Andre took the aisle seat.

About twenty students dotted the musty, poorly lit room. I watched Toni Harris chat with Mr. Rice and Ms. Hahn. I whispered to Andre that she was "the kowtow queen." Andre ignored my comment and jokingly referred to Hahn and Rice as "the odd couple." The description fit. Ms. Hahn was tall, striking, and passionate, while Mr. Rice was short, roundish, and soft-spoken. They made a good team.

Kallie's knee bounced up and down, driving me crazy.

"Kal!" I grabbed her leg. "This isn't brain surgery."

Kallie looked at me and grinned. "I'm not nervous," she laughed. "I'm jazzed." Kallie crossed her legs. Her knee stopped shaking, but her dangling foot vibrated.

An unseen person dimmed the houselights. The stage lit up. Then the auditorium door swung open, and afternoon sunlight streamed in. All eyes turned as Marcus entered. "I didn't know Marcus liked drama," Andre said under his breath.

"I didn't know he liked anything but his truck," I returned.

"He really came!" Kallie exclaimed excitedly. She whistled and motioned Marcus over. He squeezed past Andre and me and dropped into the seat on the other side of Kallie.

"Are you really going to try out?" Kallie asked breathlessly.

"Yep. I thought about what you said," Marcus returned in a voice that was actually friendly.

Later, I found out *what* Kallie had said to Marcus. Last Friday, while they were working on his truck, Kallie had noticed a Bible on the front seat. "Do you believe in God?" she had asked Marcus.

"Yep." His classic one-word response.

"Cool! Me too," she said. "Do you like reading the Bible?"

"Sometimes."

She told Marcus that she thought that was great. She liked reading scriptures too. They had that in common. It was awesome. Then she told him she was going to try out for *The Winter's Tale.* "You should too!" she invited. "Reading Shakespeare isn't much harder than reading Psalms." He said he would think about it. To me, Marcus's appearance in the auditorium seemed as strange as a biblical miracle, as wondrous as the parting of the Red Sea.

A few more people trailed in. Then Mr. Rice welcomed everybody. Ms. Hahn started calling people up one by one to audition.

Andre was the third person on stage. He walked back and forth, his body slender and lean, his voice clear and anguished as he read Leontes's words. Andre Sousa could be anyone he wanted to be onstage. My foot wasn't pumping up and down like Kallie's, but my heart was racing. When Andre finished, Toni Harris stood up and stretched her arms around his neck, hugging him. It made me sick. Andre came and sat back down. I grinned and gave him a thumbs-up.

Toni tried out for the part of Hermione, Leontes's wife.

She was small and simpering, fake all the way through. Her thick red hair was her sole positive feature.

"Toni did pretty good," Andre said quietly after she finished.

"You really think so?" I was incredulous.

"Yeah," Andre said. Then he added, "You're prejudiced against her, Trace. She's not so bad. You should give her a chance."

I shrugged.

I was glad when it was Kallie's turn, because it took my mind off Toni. Kallie smiled brightly, and each line sounded clear and full of expression. I glanced at Marcus to note his reaction. He watched Kallie intently, his features etched in granite, unreadable.

Marcus was one of the last people in the spotlight. He stood stiffly as he read the lines. But the cadence of his voice surprised me. It was musical, rich and deep. " 'The fixture of her eye has motion in't,' " he read, " 'as we are mocked with art. . . . No settled senses of the world can match the pleasure of that madness.' "

As Marcus spoke, I noticed that Kallie's foot had quit bouncing. Her smile shone as warm and bright as morning. It occurred to me that the lines Marcus had chosen might be meant for her.

As the week wore on, I got to know Marcus better. The very next day, he ate lunch with Andre, Kallie, and me. He was still quiet, but he was there. A phenomenal improvement!

Then, on Thursday afternoon during Government, I found out more about Marcus. It began with a discussion about Proposition 209. Proposition 209 was written to shoot down affirmative action, to stop the quotas guaranteeing minorities a percentage of spots in universities and the workforce. It was a volatile issue in California. I wondered how Kallie and Marcus, the only two black people in the class, felt about it.

During the first part of our class discussion, the comments were all in favor of 209. The students felt that affirmative action was wrong and unfair—that individuals shouldn't be hired or get into college because of race or gender. It wasn't a valid reason to give anyone a break. I noticed that Kallie was unusually quiet. This surprised me. She usually had strong feelings about every subject.

Then Marcus raised his hand. He spoke quietly and simply. He talked about slavery and Jim Crow laws. He asked a question. Was it wrong for people who had been pushed back for two hundred years to get a break? He was against 209, against taking away their chance.

After he finished, hands shot up. Mr. Jenson took a bunch of comments. Some of them were jabs at Marcus. Jenson just let them go.

Even though I was in favor of 209, I felt sorry for Marcus. He had finally voiced an opinion, just to have it slammed back into his face. Marcus looked straight ahead, his jaw set, his face masklike once more.

Then Brice Miller spoke up. "Maybe some payback *is* fair play," he called out. "I'm with Marcus. I'm eighteen, and I'm votin' no on 209." I could have hugged Brice, despite his purple hair. I was so glad that someone had stuck up for Marcus.

That night, Kallie called me. Her voice sounded jubilant. "Trace, I asked Marcus to homecoming, and he said yes! Ask Andre, and we'll go as a foursome! It'll be awesome!"

"What about Andre Deficit Disorder?" I mimicked Kallie's past advice. " 'Tracy, date other people! Expand your horizons.' "

Kallie cracked up. "Come on! You guys are friends! Ask him! Unless there's someone else you'd rather go with. That would be even better."

"You know there's nobody else," I sighed. I lay in bed that night trying to decide whether or not to ask Andre. How would he feel if he knew how I felt about him? Would it shred our friendship?

When I awoke the next morning, dark clouds crowded the sky. By the time seminary was over, they were dumping torrents of rain.

"Hey, Emerald Eyes! Want a ride to school?" Brice grabbed me after the closing prayer.

I hesitated. I was trying to figure out which was worse—going with Brice or the drowned-rat look. Then I thought of how Brice had stood by Marcus. "Sure," I smiled at him.

"That was nice of you to stand up for Marcus yesterday," I mentioned as we climbed into the Millers' beat-up sedan. It had a bench seat, so I put my backpack between us.

"I wasn't standing up for him," Brice said as he pushed his sopping purple bangs out of his eyes. "I agreed with him."

Brice started the car. He grinned at me and chanted, "Windshield wipers work wiping windows, but worn windshield wipers won't work wiping windows. Say that five times fast." Brice flipped on the dilapidated wipers. "Come on, Emerald Eyes, say it five times fast," he prodded.

"The name's Tracy." I sighed and tried Brice's tongue twister. I ended up with "Warm wiping wimples won't wipe winnows," and my mouth felt like fish lips. I laughed.

"Ya gotta love laughing ladies with lovely, long, lengthy locks! Try that!" Brice peered intently into the rain. I didn't respond, but I had to admit that Brice was creative.

A few minutes later, Brice found a parking place in the student lot and turned off the car. He suddenly turned his head and looked at me. "Tracy," he blurted, "there's something I want to ask you." Brice paused. I felt my face redden. Please don't ask me out, my thoughts shouted. I don't want to hurt your feelings.

Perhaps Brice saw what was behind my eyes, because he suddenly muttered, "Never mind." Then he jumped out of the car and raced around to my door. His trench coat flew in the wind as he nearly wiped out in the rain. He opened the door for me. I noticed that the purple color was dripping from his hair and smearing on his forehead. He offered me his hand as if I were a princess. I shouldered my backpack and cheerfully told Brice I was an independent nineties woman. I refused his hand and entered the downpour.

Chapter 7

THE TASTE OF SALT

By the end of second period, the rain had slowed to a heavy drizzle. People huddled to and from classes. Andre met me at my locker. The overhang partially protected us from the rain.

"Guess what," he grinned. "I got the part! I'm Leontes!"

"Glad to meet you, Leontes." I smiled and held out my right hand. "I'm Drenched."

Andre's hand was warm while mine was ice cold. "Hi, Drenched," he said. We pumped hands, and he added, "Kallie got the part of Paulina."

"Yes!" I exclaimed as we high-fived. I liked the fact that Shakespeare's Paulina was wise and strong—like Kallie. "Who else got parts?" I questioned.

"Marcus is Polixenes. It's a pretty big part. I still can't believe he tried out."

"Guess what *I* found out about Marcus and Kallie?" I asked brightly. Andre shrugged, mystified. I shifted my weight and plunged in. "Just a week ago, I told Kallie to give up on Marcus, that getting together with him was as impossible as nailing jello to a tree. Now they're going to homecoming. Can you believe it? I guess you never know what will happen."

Andre looked away without a comment. Water pooled on

the sidewalk and soaked through my tennis shoes as silence pooled between us. I suddenly felt stupid. *Now* was definitely not the time to ask him to homecoming. "Who got the part of Hermione?" I asked, seeking safer ground.

"Toni Harris."

The ground shattered under me, but I acted as if I didn't care. "Poor you. Condolences on your marriage," I teased lightly.

"Stop it, Trace. Toni's OK," Andre defended her.

I shrugged. Why was he so edgy? Didn't he understand that it was hard for me to accept the fact that Toni got the lead, that she would be the queen, the wife of Leontes, the counterpart of Andre?

"Trace, there's some stuff I want to talk to you about. Let's go get pizza tonight." Andre sounded serious.

"Sounds great," I said brightly. The second bell rang and we stepped out into the drizzle. "What stuff do you want to talk about?"

"Just some stuff," he smiled. I noticed rain droplets beading up on his long eyelashes. He meant so much to me. *What* did he want to talk to me about, and would I ever have the nerve to ask him to homecoming? Was it remotely possible that he might want to ask me?

"OK," I said as we hustled away in different directions. The tardy bell rang, and I ran. On my way to class I slipped and nearly sprawled in a mud puddle, but I caught my balance just in time.

That afternoon, Andre gave me a ride home from school. Before I got out of the car, he told me that he would pick me up at six that night. "I can't wait!" I said.

"The Pizza Station isn't *that* exciting," Andre returned.

But spending time with you is, I thought, as I ran into the house with my backpack over my head, warding off the rain.

I unlocked the front door as Andre drove away. The house was quiet. I dumped my jacket and backpack in the hall closet. In the kitchen I found a note from Mom. "Tracy," the note read, "I'm at ROC with Grandpa. I'll be home soon. Love, Mom." ROC stands for Radiation Oncology Center.

About twenty minutes later, I was reading in my room when I heard Mom pull into the garage. After I finished a chapter of *Pride and Prejudice*, I went into the kitchen to talk to her.

"How's Grandpa?" I asked as Mom put a roast in the oven for dinner.

Mom smiled at me and dropped into a kitchen chair. Not even the rain or the trip to the cancer center had dampened her spirits. "The radiation is reducing the size of the largest tumor, the one that's pressing on nerves. It makes him tired, but it's worth it because it's stopping the pain."

"Will it give him more time?" I asked.

Mom shook her head. Suddenly, her smile seemed oddly out of place. I wanted to ask Mom how much longer, but I couldn't.

A few minutes later I went into Grandpa's room. He was sound asleep. I stroked his forehead and held his hand. I thought about how he had taught me to dance, how he had taught me the gospel. I was with him when he had his heart attack two years before. I had called the ambulance. I had helped him. I couldn't help him now. I kissed his cheek. He opened his eyes and smiled at me before falling back to sleep. It reminded me of Kallie's niece, Leticia. Once, when she was a newborn, I had held her while she slept, and she had given me this sudden, sleepy smile. I looked down at Grandpa. I closed my eyes, trying to squeeze away determined tears.

Grandpa was still asleep at five o'clock when Dad came home. Rob and I were at the kitchen table finishing up a game of Rook. They were Grandpa's cards. He had taught us all to play Rook as soon as we could count.

Mom busily chopped lettuce for a salad. We all jumped

when the side door to the house slammed shut. Robbie and I made eye contact. Something was wrong. Dad was the type to trip over the carpet, but he didn't yank doors off hinges.

A moment later, Dad flung himself into the kitchen. The bald spot on his head shone from either sweat or rain. His ears were bright red and so were his eyes. Mom looked up at him while Robbie and I sat there frozen.

"Lyn," Dad blurted, "you won't believe this!"

Mom wiped her hands on a dish towel. "John," she asked worriedly, "what's wrong?"

"Elvin Cunningham, the vice principal, came around after school asking teachers to sign a statement supporting an educator's right to show R-rated movies. He came to my classroom and told me he wants every teacher's signature." Dad snorted. "He said we have to present a unified front to the school board. We can't let the uneducated public push us around. You know—united we stand, divided we fall."

Dad went on: "I told Cunningham that I wasn't comfortable signing it. Sure, there are some good R-rated movies, but we need guidelines and standards to protect students from viewing violence and pornography. It appears that I'm the only faculty member who feels that way. Cunningham reminded me that I've only been teaching at Haltsburg for two years. This year they granted my request and added an AP class to my schedule. But I'm still unproven and without tenure. He said I might want to rethink my position. I can't believe this. The jerk was threatening me!"

"Dad," I cut in, "Mr. Littlejon's the principal, not Mr. Cunningham." Mr. Littlejon was soft-spoken and a good listener. He wasn't the type to threaten anybody.

"Brad Littlejon's retiring at the end of the year," Dad explained. "Elvin Cunningham hopes to take his place."

"Call the *Herald* and tell them you've been threatened," Robbie offered, trying to lighten things up. "We could sue and be millionaires."

Dad looked seriously at Rob, as if that were an option.

"John," Mom began, "you've worked so hard . . ." She stopped abruptly and swallowed. It was as if her mask fell, her smiling mask which covered her strain and exhaustion.

"Lyn," Dad said, "maybe I'm overreacting. I'll talk to Brad tomorrow. He's still the principal." A few minutes later, Dad took Robbie and me aside and asked us not to tell anyone about the conversation. He didn't want this information leaving our family. We agreed.

An hour later, the doorbell rang. From the bathroom, where I brushed on mascara, I heard Dad welcome Andre into the living room. They talked shop. Andre was in Dad's AP Physics class, and they were both scientists at heart.

"Mr. Barton," Andre said, "I brought an article about cloning to show Bart." (Andre was always bringing interesting magazine and newspaper articles over to discuss with Grandpa.) Andre went on, "With all this cloning of mammals, do you think it will happen soon with humans?"

"There's been a lot of speculation about that," Dad said thoughtfully. "I'll surf the Internet for more information. It's a fascinating area. Cloning animals could mean unimagined opportunities for genetic research. But the cloning of humans opens a Pandora's box of moral, legal, and ethical problems. It's interesting, all right!"

As they talked about DNA, I finished my makeup, thinking about what a good teacher Dad was—how he always took time to do research and answer students' questions. How could Cunningham be such a jerk?

After Andre shared the article with Grandpa, we left for the Pizza Station. I decided to leave Dad's worries and Grandpa's illness at home. I was going to enjoy tonight. Once there, Andre and I ordered a large pizza, half pineapple and Canadian bacon for me and half pepperoni and sausage for Andre.

We talked for a while about cloning and how weird it

was. We laughed about a science fiction story that Andre had written years ago. In the story a man cloned himself so he could have a son. I told Andre he was psychic; that story wasn't so far-fetched after all. We scarfed down our pizza and ordered a tray of bread sticks. It felt so good to be with Andre.

We were almost finished with the bread sticks, when I asked Andre what he specifically wanted to talk to me about.

Andre paused for a moment and took a long sip of his Coke. "It's nothing much," he began. "Yesterday, Cunningham asked me to take home a couple of videos. He wants me to talk at the school board meeting next week, to tell everybody how I feel about these movies. You know, a student's perspective."

"How do you feel?" I asked as my insides turned to ice. Andre was talking about the controversial R-rated movies. Cunningham had threatened Dad, and now he was using Andre because Andre was Haltsburg High's brightest and most eloquent student.

"Trace," Andre explained, "I watched them. They are partly about prejudice. I kept thinking about when I was a little kid and we moved here. Kids called me names because I couldn't speak English. Then, when I could understand them, they told me jokes like, 'How do you find the population of Brazil? By throwing a quarter in the street.' 'Who's the richest Brazilian? The one with the quarter.'"

"Little kids can be stupid," I said.

"Yeah," Andre said, "because they learn from their parents, from society. That's why these movies are so important. They teach people about hate and intolerance. They educate people. They open people's eyes and help them to care. But I know how your church feels about R-rated movies. Mom's not too happy about what I'm going to do. I wanted to explain to you."

Andre had said "your church," not "the church"—not a

good sign. I wanted to tell him about Dad, but I couldn't. I had promised. I tried a different way. "But, Andre," I explained, "last year Reynolds showed this horrible movie. For no reason. He just said he deserved a break that day. It was so violent! There were body parts everywhere. It was sick. I wanted to walk out, but I knew I could get suspended."

"You can't outlaw a whole category of movies because of one lousy teacher," Andre said. I was quiet. I looked at the lights outside the window. They looked fuzzy in the dark rain. I didn't know what to say. I didn't know what to do.

"Trace," Andre pled, "I can't help how I feel."

"You're on the wrong side," I said lamely.

"Trace, I just don't see things like you do. I read part of the Book of Mormon, but all I can think about is how it probably didn't happen. And the Joseph Smith story—I can't swallow it."

"You don't understand," I said. Then I remembered an object lesson from seminary. "What if I had never tasted salt and I asked you to describe it to me. You wouldn't know how. It's like that with a testimony. It's like that with faith. I don't know how to describe it."

"If you had never tasted salt, I would take you to the ocean," Andre countered. "I would tell you that salt tastes like the sea."

I looked down at the bread stick I was holding. I wasn't hungry anymore.

I looked back at Andre. "Cunningham is using you," I said levelly.

"Cunningham wants what is best for the students," Andre argued.

"No. Cunningham wants to win. He'll walk over anybody to get his way."

"Maybe this isn't about Cunningham; maybe this is about censorship, about right and wrong," Andre said.

"It's definitely about right and wrong!" I snapped.

This time, Andre looked away. He stared out the window while he said, "Tracy, there's something else I need to tell you."

"What?" I asked warily. I couldn't get Dad out of my mind. Andre picked up a bread stick. Then he put it down.

"Toni Harris asked me to homecoming," he said. "I guess I'll go. I don't want to hurt her feelings."

My heart ached. "Have fun," I lied. I didn't trust myself to say anything else. I was fighting tears. Andre cracked his knuckles and stared at me moodily. We finished eating, but our conversation was forced. When Andre took me home, he didn't walk me to the door.

As I opened the front door, Katie skidded down the hallway to meet me. "Look, Tracy!" she yelled, pointing to candy kisses which were all over the floor. Katie grabbed my hand and pulled me after her as we followed the kisses. They made a path all the way into my room. There was a big candy kiss and an envelope with my name on it on the bed. I figured that Kallie was behind this. "Can I put the kisses in a bowl and eat them?" Katie asked.

I nodded. "But save some for me," I added as Katie skipped out of the room. I opened the envelope.

"Tracy," the note began. "Notice that I did not call you Emerald Eyes. Now that I've kissed the ground you walk on, will you go to homecoming with me? Love, Brice."

Numbly, I threw down the envelope and closed the door. I curled up on my bed and buried my head in my pillow. I tried not to cry, but I couldn't help it. I know what salt tastes like, I thought bitterly. It tastes like tears.

Chapter 8

UNDERSTANDING EVERYTHING ALWAYS

I had trouble sleeping that night. It wasn't just that Andre was going to homecoming with Toni. I could deal with total disappointment. But other things haunted me. Andre's words played over and over again in my mind, "These movies teach people about hate and intolerance. They open their eyes. I read part of the Book of Mormon—but all I can think about is how it didn't happen. I don't see things the way you do."

After I finally dozed off, I awoke a short time later, shaken by a strange dream. In the dream, I relaxed in a chair in the middle of a grassy field. I was eating pizza and writing in my journal. A fire swept through the field. I dropped the pizza and the book. Then I pulled my feet up onto the chair. The fire passed, consuming the journal and the pizza, but I was OK. I was left alone surrounded by a black, charred, empty world. After that, I woke up.

I lay awake for a while trying to figure out the meaning behind my dream. Soft light from the street lamp leaked through the blinds. I heard Angel hop softly into my room. I called her, and she jumped onto my bed. Finally, I fell asleep surrounded by her smell and warmth.

I awoke at nine Saturday morning. Angel was still in bed with me. I hugged her as the sunlight streamed in. Someone had opened my blinds. Probably Mom. She's famous for running around the house and opening all the blinds in the morning. I thought about how I needed to go out to Montagues' and care for the horses. It was my job, what I was paid to do, what I loved to do. Yet, this time I dreaded going because it could mean facing Andre. I wasn't ready for that. Things still hurt too much. What was I supposed to do? Call Anita and tell her I couldn't do my job because I couldn't be around her son?

I reached for the phone near my bed and dialed Kallie's number instead. She answered, and I told her the sordid details from my evening with Andre.

"Oh, Trace," she said empathetically. "Toni was all over Andre at Thursday's rehearsal. But deep inside he loves you. I know that."

"Don't say that, Kal," I said desperately.

Kallie went on: "He's just scared because you guys are such good friends. And you have different religious beliefs. He knows it can't work out in the long run. He can't become a Mormon if he doesn't believe in God."

"Kallie, he doesn't think of me that way. He thinks of me as a friend or a mascot or something."

"No way, Trace! But maybe you should go to homecoming with Brice! It wouldn't hurt for Andre to see you looking beautiful. Go as friends. We could double. Brice can be entertaining."

"I can't, Kal," I said. "But how do I tell Brice no without hurting his feelings?"

"Tell him the truth," Kallie suggested.

"On the pathway to truth each blade of grass is a knife," I paraphrased.

"What?" Kallie asked.

"But someone with purple hair couldn't possibly have feelings. So there's nothing to worry about. Right?"

"Earth to Tracy!"

"I don't want to be on Earth. I want to find a worm hole to another universe. ADD is deadly!"

By the end of the conversation Kallie was laughing, and I knew I had enough strength to go out to Montagues' and do my job.

An hour later, I pulled up to Andre's house with Angel on the seat next to me, my moral support. Marcus was outside, washing his truck. Angel jumped out of the Honda and scampered to Marcus, her tail wagging. He bent down and put his hands on each side of her face. She licked his nose.

"I think she likes you," I said.

"I like her," Marcus returned. The sun struck his earring, and his teeth flashed white as he turned his head and smiled at me. He had a great smile. I wanted to tell him that he should smile more often.

"I'd better get to work," I said as I headed for the barn.

"See ya later, Tracy," Marcus called after me. I suddenly realized that I had never heard Marcus say my name before.

It was too muddy to go riding, so I spent the next hour and a half mucking out stalls and grooming and graining the horses. I was about ready to leave when Andre came into the barn carrying Paulo's halter.

"Hi, Trace," he said.

"Hi," I said back. Act friendly, I told myself. Act like nothing is wrong. It was quiet for a few minutes as Andre adjusted the halter.

"I was thinking about last night," Andre finally said. "Do you want to double to homecoming? I could set you up."

I stared at Andre. Didn't he understand how much he was hurting me? "No," I responded, not very graciously. "Believe it or not, someone already asked me."

"That's great! Who?"

"Never mind," I said coldly, looking away. What was I supposed to say—he has purple hair, but he's not Barney?

When I looked back at Andre, I saw frustration smoldering in his eyes. He threw down the halter. "You take everything wrong! I just didn't want you to feel left out! Some guys don't think about asking you out because you and I hang around together! Not everybody realizes we're just friends!"

"I guess I won't have to worry about that anymore! Not with Toni around!" I was losing it.

"I can't believe this!" Andre said loudly. "You used to listen! Now you're so closed minded! I thought we were best friends!"

"Maybe I'm tired of being best friends!" I hurried out of the barn.

I grabbed my dog and put her in the car. I was crying now. By the way Marcus concentrated on drying his truck, I knew he had heard every word.

As soon as I was home, I ducked into my bedroom and called Brice. "I'll go as a friend," I said into the phone. "I don't want anything else. But if you still want to go, I'll go."

"I want to go," Brice said. For once he sounded serious.

"Well, good-bye," I said.

"See you at church tomorrow," Brice added. "I won't forget. Just friends."

"Thanks, Brice," I said.

"For what?"

"For understanding."

"Big bad Brice understands everything always," Brice answered with a tongue twister. I didn't laugh. The afternoon had drained all humor from me.

"I wish I did," I said to myself more than to Brice.

"Did what?"

"Understand everything always."

"I wish you did too," Brice said quietly before saying good-bye and hanging up the phone.

Chapter 9

Emerald City

A few minutes later, Katie ran into my bedroom. Her blond curls bounced as she jumped up and down like a pogo stick.

"Tracy!" she squealed. "Kallie called while you were gone! It's *Wizard of Oz* day! She invited us over! Me and you! Her cousins my age are coming. Her mom's going to make fudge. She'll start making it at the beginning of the movie, and it will be finished when Dorothy reaches Emerald City! Can we go?"

"Why not?" I mumbled. Maybe a distraction would ease the ache inside me. Katie skipped to her room, not noticing that my eyes were red.

Two hours later, when Katie and I arrived at the Thompsons', Danika opened the door, with her baby, Leticia, balanced on her hip.

"Hey, girl." Danika stepped out onto the porch and hugged me with her spare arm. Leticia grabbed my thumb and stuck it into her mouth.

"I hear things aren't going too well with Andre Boy," Danika said as she guided me into the house. Then she added, "Girl, take it from me, men aren't worth your tears!" Once we were inside, Danika deposited Leticia on the floor and hugged Katie, exclaiming, "Katie Baby, you're so big now!"

I heard the garage door open, and in seconds a group of people, including Kallie and her mom, crowded into the small kitchen. "Trace!" Kallie flung her arm around me. "I'm so glad you came. We do this each year. Mom is the original *Wizard of Oz* fan."

Kallie's mom, Sidney, a large-boned black woman with wiry long hair, clunked a bag of fudge-making ingredients on the counter. Then she bent down and kissed Katie on the cheek. "You beautiful little angel," she said warmly. "We're glad you came to visit us!"

Sidney introduced us to her sister, Sarah, and Sarah's twin boys. Sarah was smaller and more compact than Sidney. Her seven-year-old boys, Stanley and Steven, looked identical with their dark skin, close-cropped hair, skinny legs, huge eyes, and big toothy grins.

The twins immediately asked Katie to play *Star Wars* with them until the movie started. Katie was delighted. She twirled around, Princess Leia in person. In moments, the three tore circles through the house, the boys screaming with laughter because the princess couldn't tell which twin was Darth Vader and which was Luke Skywalker. To solve the problem, Katie drew her lightsaber and killed them both.

"Yes!" Danika cheered as the twins writhed on the kitchen floor. "Good triumphs over evil! Woman destroys man!" Leticia erupted into baby giggles.

Aunt Sarah scolded Danika good-naturedly. "Girl, stop your men bashing! Just 'cause you picked a bad apple the first time doesn't mean the whole bag is rotten!"

A little while later, Danika turned on the movie, and the kids flopped down in front of the TV. Then Kallie, Danika, and I went into the kitchen to help with the fudge. I felt strangely apart as I watched Kal and her family work together. They bantered back and forth affectionately, cracking jokes and slapping each other on the back. They were so free and relaxed. I thought about Mom, Casey, and me. We loved each other, but we didn't laugh as much. Maybe there was more distance between us.

"Tracy, Kallie told us you've had a bad day," Sidney's voice interrupted my thoughts. "Come over here, honey, and beat the fudge. You'll feel better." I took the sturdy wooden spoon and beat the fudge until my arm ached.

When Dorothy reached Emerald City the fudge was done. Sidney brought a tray into the family room, and, as Danika put it, we ate until our guts ached. After that, Aunt Sarah and Danika played cards with the kids, while Kallie and I went into the kitchen to help Sidney wash up.

While Kallie and I washed dishes, Sidney addressed me as if Kallie wasn't right there beside us. "Tracy, honey, my Kallie's like Dorothy on the yellow brick road. Your Mormon church is her Emerald City. She wants to be baptized so bad! But the Reverend Marshall told me that Mormons aren't Christians."

"Mom!" Kallie cut in, exasperated. "Not now!"

"Hush, Kallie, I'm talking to Tracy." Sidney continued, "Anyway, I read the Book of Mormon last week. It's about Jesus. If Mormonism is still Kallie's Emerald City, I'm through standing between her and the city gate."

"Are you serious, Mom?" Kallie sounded like she was afraid to breathe. "Can I really get baptized?"

"Yea, baby, you can," Sidney said softly as she turned to Kallie. Kallie hugged her mom with tears in her eyes. I had tears in my eyes too. But my tears weren't solely tears of joy for Kallie; they were also tears of sadness because Andre believed that Mormonism was as much a fairy tale as the Land of Oz, because no matter how hard I tried not to, I couldn't help listening to him.

Sunday dawned. The wind blew, making way for another storm. Mom was sick. She had been awake most of the night coughing. Before Dad left for bishopric meeting, he came into my room. "Tracer," he said as he rumpled my hair. (I figured he'd rumple my hair at my wedding reception.) Dad continued, "Mom's staying home this morning. Will you get Rob and Katie to church?"

"Sure," I said. "No problem."

"No problem" ended up being the biggest understatement on earth. When I attempted to brush Katie's hair, she shrieked that I was killing her. To make matters worse, she decided to wear a tacky neon-green dress lined with plastic netting. It ballooned out like a parachute. Mom had purchased it at a garage sale for Katie's most recent Halloween costume. Katie tearfully insisted that she wear the dress, and I, the official wimp of the world, gave in.

Then a bare-chested Robbie ran out of his room, yelling that he couldn't find his shirt and tie. His baggy pants stayed up only because of his belt. I looked at the clock. It would be a miracle if we made it to sacrament meeting.

After a desperate search, we located Rob's clothes—wadded in Angel's box. Before Rob put them on, I shook out the shirt and brushed off the dog hairs. If he left his jacket on, maybe no one would notice. Then I braided my hair, threw on an old sweater, a denim skirt, and boots. I surveyed us. We resembled an unlikely trio of orphans from *The Wizard of Oz.* Rob could pass as a scarecrow, Katie had the appearance of a resident of Emerald City, and I looked almost as dorky as Dorothy.

We were about to walk out the door, when Grandpa emerged from his room. He said he felt well enough to go with us. He looked very thin and brave with his suit hanging on him and his moustache trimmed.

Fifteen minutes later, we slipped into the chapel, right after the opening song and prayer. Dad watched us from his seat next to the bishop. He pushed his glasses up. His eyes widened slightly in surprise when he saw Grandpa. Dad's tie was crooked, and he smiled paternally at me. Then, as we sat down, Katie's dress rustled so loudly that the whole row of deacons snickered.

A moment later, Bishop Leriway took the stand. He welcomed everyone to fast and testimony meeting. He explained that fast Sunday was a week late due to the recent general conference. Then he made an announcement. The following week's school board meeting would include a discussion of the R-rated movies that were being shown at the high school. It would be an open discussion that the public was invited to participate in. Bishop Leriway encouraged a strong showing from the ward, emphasizing that it was an opportunity for both parents and students to stand for the right.

After that, the bishop bore his testimony and invited others to come to the microphone. I usually liked testimony meetings, but this day was different. It felt like I watched from a distance. It was as if I saw everything from Andre's point of view. Questions and doubts flooded my mind.

Sister Stevens stood up and tearfully said that Heavenly Father told her where her car keys were. She was able to get her cat, who was having convulsions, to the vet in time to save its life. Then why wasn't Grandpa's cancer found in time? I thought grimly. Are cats more important to God than grandfathers?

Then Brother Kabisky mentioned a special on TV that referred to people as children of evolution. He said he knew that wasn't true; he testified that we were children of God. I remembered Andre telling me that our backbones and spinal cords indicate that we evolved from apes. He also once told me that we were made of star dust. How did it fit together? Where was the truth?

Janie Londermack, who is half Navajo, stood up. She was thankful to be a literal descendant of Lehi. But how could she be sure that her ancestors didn't come across the Bering Strait? I sat cold and still, bombarded by my thoughts. My faith was crumbling, and I wasn't strong enough to stop it.

Then Grandpa got up and slowly made his way to the front of the chapel. He climbed the stairs and stood at the podium. The bishop pushed a button that electronically lowered the podium, adjusting the height for Grandpa.

Grandpa's testimony wasn't very long. He said that he knew God lived, that he was thankful for life. Faith wasn't just wishful thinking but something very real. "The Apostle Paul used the words *substance* and *evidence* to describe faith," Grandpa explained. "It's the '*substance* of things hoped for, the *evidence* of things not seen.' " Grandpa said he was thankful that the Savior's atonement was infinite and eternal, that we would all someday return to the God who gave us life.

As Grandpa made his way down from the stand, so frail and dear, something snapped inside of me. I felt sobs gathering. I hurried from the chapel and ducked into the bathroom. I turned on the sink and gripped the side as I willed myself *not* to cry.

"Trace, are you OK?" I heard Kallie's voice behind me and felt her hand on my shoulder.

I didn't turn around. I just mumbled something about Andre not believing that the Church was true and about my grandpa dying.

"Trace, it'll be OK," Kallie said. I took a few deep breaths and washed my face.

"Come on," Kallie said after I had calmed down. "There's something in the foyer you have to see!"

I followed her out. The only thing in the foyer was a guy I didn't know who had short blond hair and a dark suit. He sat on one of the sofas. Kallie walked straight towards him. As we drew near, recognition stopped me short.

"Brice?" I stammered, truly stunned.

Brice laughed at me. "Halloween's coming. I thought I would go as a normal person."

"You look great!" Kallie said as she dropped down next to him. Then she added, "Guess what, Bricey. I'm getting baptized the second Saturday in November!"

"What a bomb!" Brice put his arm around her. "Can I come?"

"Sure. If you wear your Halloween costume," Kallie returned.

I sank down next to Kallie. Kallie's comment struck me as wackily funny. Brice would look normal if he wore his Halloween costume. Maybe he would wear his Halloween costume to the homecoming dance. Was it possible that I wouldn't end up going with the cross between a sixties flower child, a punk rocker, and Barney? Suddenly I cracked up. It felt so good to laugh.

The organ in the chapel began the closing song, "I Know That My Redeemer Lives." Kallie sang along softly with her gorgeous alto voice. She squeezed my hand. Her braids brushed against my shoulder. I felt her strength and her friendship. I no longer felt as alone or as confused.

Chapter 10

CLOUT AND CLASS

That evening I went into Grandpa's room. He had fallen asleep with his reading glasses on and a large book on his chest. It was titled *Unifying the Quantum Theory with General Relativity*. When I lifted the book I found Grandpa's scriptures underneath it. They were open too.

"Tracy," Grandpa said. "I was just dozing." He nodded towards the book on relativity. "Andre lent me this a couple of months ago. I'm finally getting around to reading it." Grandpa pushed his glasses up and motioned for me to sit next to him.

Suddenly, I found myself telling Grandpa all about my weekend. I told him about my conversations with Andre, about my lack of faith, about my fears.

"Honey," Grandpa said when I finished, "I don't know which is more difficult—growing up or growing old. But try not to worry about the things we simply don't understand yet. To Andre, science and religion are opposing forces. But to me, knowledge men have gained through creative study and knowledge revealed by God are both compelling areas of truth. They work in perfect harmony even if we don't completely comprehend how. They are like the front and back of the same hand, God's hand."

That night, I borrowed the book Andre had lent Grandpa.

I read it until I fell asleep. I dreamt about quantum theory, black holes, and alternative time sequences.

My radio woke me up early the next morning. The six o'clock weather brimmed with dire warnings. The storm door had broken open, and we were in the middle of another record-breaking deluge. This kind of rain was unheard of at this time of year. Residents should beware and prepare for flooding. I flipped off the news, but I couldn't escape the sound of the rain beating on the roof.

After I dressed and braided my hair, I went to the kitchen and found Dad scrambling eggs. As we ate breakfast, Dad told me that Mom was running a fever of 102. The Van Horns had called and said they wouldn't be picking me up for seminary. Dad offered to give me a ride.

On the way to the church, I asked how things were going for Dad. His confidential tone surprised me. It was as if I were his friend rather than his daughter.

"I'm uptight about the school board meeting tomorrow night," Dad sighed as he peered through the windshield wipers into the dark, sopping morning. "It's going to be an open forum discussion where the public takes the floor. Bishop Leriway asked me to make some comments. Supposedly, a teacher who's opposed to R-rated movies has some clout."

I looked over at Dad. He wasn't the "clout" type. He was the overgrown puppy type. I asked Dad if he had talked to Mr. Littlejon yet, if there was any danger of losing his job.

"I talked to Brad yesterday," Dad shared as he let go of the steering wheel and pushed up his glasses with both hands. Our car headed towards oncoming traffic. Dad grabbed the wheel and swerved. A passing van flashed its brights and honked savagely.

I gripped the dash. "Dad," I said when we were safely back in our own lane, "did you know the number of accidents increases in rainy weather?"

Dad seemed to miss the point. Then he continued, "Anyway, Mr. Littlejon understands my point of view. But he's retiring, and the superintendent plans to promote Elvin. That's the reason Brad is letting Elvin call the shots. Brad told me that he feels I'm an excellent teacher and that he'll discuss things with Elvin." Dad sighed, "I don't look forward to Elvin's promotion. I'm starting out on his bad side, and things could be pretty uncomfortable next year."

"I wouldn't worry, Dad," I said. "Cunningham's probably really scared of you. You have access to dissecting knives and all those chemicals."

Dad laughed out loud. We both knew that Dad was about as dangerous as Mr. Rogers. Except when he was at the wheel.

"Tracer," he said as the Honda bumped over the curb into the church's parking lot, "I'm coming home early today so I'll give you a lift after sixth period."

"Don't you have faculty meeting?"

"I'm not going." Dad shrugged, then smiled a bit ruefully. "Elvin will think I'm either really mad or really chicken. But the truth is that I have to take Grandpa to his radiation treatment. Your mother's not up to it."

As I climbed out of the car, I thought about Dad. Landing the job in Haltsburg and teaching AP Physics and Advanced Chemistry were his dreams. Now those dreams were thin ice under his feet. But he smiled kindly and laughed at my jokes even as the ice cracked. My dad might not have class or clout, but he had courage.

Later in the day, I thought of Dad's courage as I sloshed into AP English with my braids dripping. Andre and Toni sat together. Somehow Toni had managed to keep her hair dry despite the wind and rain. She turned towards me and flashed a fake, overly friendly smile.

Andre motioned for me to come sit in an empty seat on his other side. I shook my head and sat by Tricia Otto, a nice girl with dark hair, glasses, and a lisp.

Ms. Hahn briefly mentioned the school board meeting and invited students to attend and voice opinions on either side of the movie issue. She smiled at me when she said "either side of the issue." Toni leaned into Andre and whispered something. He nodded. It made me sick.

Then I suddenly remembered Danika once saying that breaking a drug addiction was incredibly painful, like running through sheets of glass every second. Resolve hardened within me. I would break my addiction. I would shatter ADD.

I focused on what Ms. Hahn said. She spoke animatedly about an immoral society manipulating Hardy's Tess. It was immoral of Cunningham to try to manipulate my dad! After class, I didn't even answer when Andre called my name.

It was chilly and clouds covered the moon Tuesday night when Dad and I drove to the district office building in downtown Haltsburg. As we walked through the double doors into the school board meeting, Sister Dawson handed us stickers to wear. Each sticker had a red circle with a black line slashing through a capital *R*.

The room was packed. Half the ward was there. I saw Pastor Smith from the Baptist church. Teachers were scattered throughout the crowd. Cunningham and Littlejon sat together. Andre was near the front by Ms. Hahn and Grant. Anita hadn't come.

Bishop Leriway came up to us and put his arm on Dad's shoulder. "I've saved seats for you!" He shook our hands and smiled.

"OK, then," Dad said a bit uncomfortably as we made our way down the aisle.

A moment later, the school superintendent called the meeting to order. Fifteen minutes of miscellaneous business followed. Then he smiled like a politician and said that the time was at hand to discuss the policy of movies in classrooms. Commotion erupted. People stood up, yelling, "No Rs! No Rs!"

The superintendent quieted the crowd. He explained that currently there was no policy outlining what could and could not be shown in high school classrooms. He invited a tall brunette woman, Mrs. Gray, from the district's curriculum planning committee to speak.

Mrs. Gray said that she empathized with parents. The district was proposing a new policy to the school board. This proposal required teachers to be responsible by outlining any movies they planned to show in a syllabus which would be given to parents at the beginning of the year. There would be a designated evening on which parents could come to the district office to preview the movies. The syllabus would contain a form that parents could sign and return to the school if they didn't want their children to see any R-rated movies for religious or personal reasons. These students would be given other assignments in place of watching the movies.

As she spoke, people yelled things like "Not good enough!" "No Rs at all!" and "Protect all kids!" After she sat down, the yells and heckling increased. The superintendent stood up, red-faced. "We are going to open up the floor for discussion," he said sternly. "And I expect you to listen to each other with respect, the kind of respect we require from the students in our district."

"We'll show *you* respect when you respect our children's rights—their right not to be exposed to pornography, profanity, and violence!" screamed a voice. It was Sister Miller, Brice's mom. She looked even more angry and pinched than usual. Her husband, a tired-looking man with an elongated face, stared at the superintendent. Brice wasn't with them. Bishop Leriway looked down. I think he was embarrassed by the rudeness. I wondered how Dad felt.

The superintendent ignored Sister Miller and said calmly, "Now we'll open the floor for discussion. You may line up at the microphone. Each person has up to two minutes. I implore you to listen with respect."

About thirty people lined up to speak, including ten people from our ward as well as Ms. Hahn, Andre, and Dad. Some of the people on both sides spoke politely and eloquently, but others were vindictive and threatening.

Ms. Hahn spoke about the historical dangers of fanaticism and censorship. She talked about the need to give children knowledge and truth, even if that included a handful of outstanding R-rated films.

When Andre's turn came, he read the poem by Stephen Crane about the wayfarer on the pathway to truth. The wayfarer turns away from the truth because of the knives along the path. After reading the poem, Andre talked about how the teachers were courageous in choosing the pathway to truth by showing excellent films that taught students about life, that taught them truth. Even though there were horribly graphic things in the films, like knives along the way, it was important for students to know what the real world was like, the world that past generations had handed to them.

After Andre finished speaking, there was scattered clapping that was interrupted by a loud undercurrent of disagreement from the audience. Andre sat down, never looking in my direction.

A few minutes later, it was Dad's turn. Dad looked tall, soft, and clumsy at the microphone. He pushed his glasses up—the absent-minded professor. I didn't know if people would take Dad seriously. But as Dad introduced himself, the room quieted.

Dad talked about teachers like Ms. Hahn and how hard they worked, how difficult it was to deal with the harsh problems of teens, and how constant the scrutiny of the public eye was. Such teachers thoughtfully planned their curriculum. They were dedicated to their students. He had great respect for their abilities and their points of view. He valued their friendship.

Yet, as a teacher and as a parent he favored a "no R"

policy. He felt a need to protect students. Then, referring to Andre's comments, Dad said, "I have spent my whole life trying to help my students and my own children along the pathway to truth and knowledge. I don't want to blind them by protecting them. But if I can I will reach down and pull out some of the knives so that their path to truth will be smoother and less painful. I want to protect them from graphic violence and pornography. I know they will see the ugliness of the world, but I don't want to force it in front of their eyes. I want to guide them towards maturity and inner strength. I think any policy that allows the showing of R-rated movies will hurt more children than it helps. I hope the school board will listen."

After Dad finished, clapping thundered through the room. Dad lumbered back to his seat beside me. The bishop whispered, "Thank you, John."

Ten minutes later, when the superintendent closed the meeting, he said that the board needed more time to discuss the proposed policy. He looked at Mr. Littlejon and added, "Until there is a clear policy in place, please ask your teachers to refrain from showing R-rated movies."

Mr. Littlejon smiled kindly and nodded. "Yes, sir." But Cunningham's face was red.

After the meeting, Dad was anxious to get home. But people in the ward kept stopping him as we tried to make our way to the door. Sister Miller clapped him on the back. "Good work, John!" she exclaimed. Just then Andre walked by, staring straight ahead.

Dad immediately turned from the Millers and clumsily reached for Andre, touching his elbow. Andre spun around. There was hurt in his eyes. "Son," Dad said seriously, "you did a good job up there. You handled yourself well in front of a hostile audience."

The look in Andre's eyes softened as he focused on Dad. "So did you, Mr. Barton," he returned levelly. As Andre walked away, the Millers looked at Dad like he had a split personality.

As we drove home, I sat quietly, deep in thought. Occasionally, I gazed at my dad. How could I have known him all my life and misjudged him so completely? How many times had I been embarrassed by his gawky kindness, his social incorrectness? Now I realized how blind I had been. Not only did my dad have courage, but he had clout and class too.

Chapter 11

HEAVY CLOUDS

The following morning, the sky was so bright and clear that yesterday's storm warnings seemed impossible. But by the end of third period, heavy clouds crowded the horizon. By noon, the storm was in full swing.

During lunch, I squeezed into the packed cafeteria and shouldered my way to a table where Kallie was sitting with Marcus and Brice. They were discussing an opinion paper we had to write for Government. Should marijuana be legalized for medicinal use as proposed on the November ballot?

"It's confusing," Kallie said passionately. "I don't think anything should be illegal that helps cancer and AIDS victims. At least it shouldn't be illegal for *them*."

"If you let people grow it for medicine you might as well legalize pot, because somebody's gonna use the leftovers," Brice said lightly. "Besides alcohol *is* legal, and it's just as bad."

"This law allows people to use pot with just a doctor's verbal permission. It's unenforceable," Marcus began. "It's asking for trouble. If it's medicine, it should be controlled and go through a pharmacy just like painkillers." I could tell that Marcus felt that his opinion was the only opinion.

"What do you think, Tracy?" Kallie asked.

"Marcus sounds right," I said simply. "But I don't know

much about marijuana." It was the truth. I was a senior in high school, and I had never broken the Word of Wisdom, not even a drink of iced tea. Deep inside, I was glad, but sometimes I felt about as naive as a five-year-old.

"Hey!"

I heard Andre's voice behind me. I turned. Toni was glued to his side, her hand in his hip pocket.

As we exchanged greetings, I forced a smile. I was determined to be friendly without feeling anything. Brice sipped his soda, following Andre's every move with his eyes.

"Trace, I have a message for you," Andre said. "Your dad wants to talk to you in his classroom."

"Thanks," I said, avoiding eye contact.

"People," Toni cut in, "rehearsal is canceled today because of some surprise faculty meeting. If you want, we could meet at my house after school and practice on our own. You could come too, Tracy, and watch."

I'd rather be crushed between two semitrucks, I thought. But I kept my thoughts to myself. I was about to gracefully decline when Brice interrupted.

"Do I exist?" He looked directly at Toni. "Am I included in this invitation?"

"Brice, you're included," Toni said sweetly. "It's just that I didn't recognize you. Your hair's *different.*"

"For Halloween," Brice said simply.

"Brice is going as a normal person," Kallie explained.

"Oh, I thought you had changed your hair for homecoming next week. I hear you have a hot date." Toni smiled conspiratorially at me.

I felt Kallie lay a hand on my knee. She was telling me to cool down, to take a deep breath, to refrain from saying something I'd regret for the rest of my life.

Then Andre added quickly, "I can't come this afternoon, Toni."

"Andre, I know you're not scheduled to work." Toni took

her hand out of his pocket and entwined her fingers through his. Her nail polish was the same color as her hair. "Why can't you come?"

"A doctor appointment," Andre said.

" 'Dre, are you sick?" Toni laid her other hand on Andre's forehead. I stood up and shouldered my backpack. I couldn't stomach any more.

"Trace, where are you going?" Kallie looked up at me. Our eyes met. Where was I going? Outside to cry in the rain? Then I remembered what Andre had told me.

"My dad wants to talk to me," I said shortly. I hurried through the rainy outdoor corridors, hating Toni with every step.

A few minutes later I stood in the doorway of Dad's classroom. He slept at his desk, his head buried in lab notebooks.

I cleared my throat.

Dad looked up at me and yawned. He lifted his head, pushed up his glasses, and smiled like Goofy.

"What's up?" I asked.

"I need your help, sweetheart."

"How?" I pushed away a stack of tests and took a seat on his desk.

"I'm supposed to take Grandpa to radiation today, but this morning Mr. Littlejon announced another faculty meeting right after school. In my current situation, I'm afraid to duck out. Do you need to work at Montagues' this afternoon?"

"No, I'll stay home and watch Katie. I don't feel like mucking out stalls in this weather."

"The trouble is that Rob and Katie have dentist appointments this afternoon," Dad continued. "Katie's getting her first filling and is scared to death. Mom needs to be there. Could you take Grandpa?"

"OK," I said hesitantly as I sucked in a deep breath and thought of my splintered day. The cancer center was in

Sacramento. It was raining hard, and I didn't know my way. Fingers of fear squeezed my stomach.

Dad scribbled something on a piece of paper. It was a hand-drawn map showing me how to get to the cancer center. "You probably won't need this because Grandpa knows the way," he added reassuringly.

I took the map and put it in my backpack. Dad reached into his lunch bag and handed me half of a sandwich made from yesterday's pot roast.

"Thanks," I said as I took a bite.

"Thank *you*, Tracer." Dad rumpled my hair. "By the way, the appointment's at 4:00, and Andre is going with you."

"Dad, I don't think so," I said slowly, looking down at my blunt fingernails. Then I explained, "Andre and I haven't exactly been getting along lately."

"Tracer, try not to be angry at Andre for things he doesn't understand," Dad said gently, referring to the school board meeting.

"Dad," I added, "he has a girlfriend now. I don't think he *wants* to go with us."

"Trace," Dad said, "Andre loves your grandfather too. I talked to him after class. He offered to go."

I looked at my dad, but in my mind I pictured all the times Andre and I had shared with Grandpa. Then I remembered how Dad used to worry about my relationship with Andre. Two years before, he wanted us to stop spending time together. He didn't trust Andre and was afraid I might get hurt. Now I was hurt. But Dad wasn't worried anymore. It's strange how things change. But you can't make them stay the same. You can't nail jello to a tree. I sighed.

"Daddy," I said hesitantly. "There's one other thing. I'm afraid of the cancer center. I'm afraid of the people there. Of the disease. I don't know if I can deal with it."

"I was too," Dad said as he patted my knee. "But it's a beautiful facility. A powerful house of healing."

A long time ago, Dad had used the same phrase to describe the temple—a powerful house of healing, spiritual healing. I thought about Grandpa. I didn't want him to miss a treatment. I wanted his life to be as long and as free from pain as possible. I was a part of him, and he was a part of me. We were sealed together. Forever.

"OK, Dad," I said. "I'll go with Grandpa. Andre can come along."

Chapter 12

A House of Healing

It was raining hard, and the traffic thickened as we neared Sacramento. Grandpa sat in the front seat next to me, and Andre was in the back. The windshield wipers weren't working very well, and my head ached. In my mind, I dismally repeated Brice's tongue twister—worn windshield wipers won't work wiping windows.

Suddenly, Andre leaned up from the backseat and stuck his head between mine and Grandpa's. "Hey, Bart," he said cheerfully, "Tracy's taking her time. I hear they radiate an extra toe for each second you're late."

Grandpa chuckled. "They radiate my tongue if we're over fifteen minutes late," he teased.

"You guys stop," I said, trying to be cheerful for Grandpa's sake. "I'm driving as fast as I can."

I felt nervous, though. The weather was terrible, and Grandpa was fragile. What if he got really sick after the treatment? What if I couldn't find a place to park and he became soaked and chilled in the rain?

"Here's our exit," I said with a smile. I was turning into Mom, acting happy when I felt lousy.

Grandpa smiled back. "Go past Capital and turn left on L Street. There's valet parking."

We approached the Sacramento Cancer Center, a towering building next to the hospital. I pulled into a circular driveway near the entrance. A great-looking guy in a yellow rain slicker took my keys. Andre helped Grandpa out. Clear glass doors opened for us. We didn't get wet.

We took the elevator downstairs to Radiation Oncology. The lights were bright. The waiting area, a large carpeted room decorated in greens and blues, was pretty. It included lots of green plants and an indoor waterfall. There were sofas, soft chairs, and tables with puzzles on them.

About twenty people sat around reading or chatting quietly. I noticed an elegant lady in a bright turban working on a puzzle. She didn't have any eyebrows or eyelashes. But everyone else looked normal. All in all, it was a peaceful place. I guess I had imagined bald people huddled together weeping.

The receptionist smiled warmly and apologetically at Grandpa. She explained that the B machine was behind schedule, and it would be a thirty-minute wait.

We sat down, with Andre and I on opposite sides of Grandpa. Andre worked on a puzzle. Grandpa closed his eyes and rested. After fifteen minutes, Grandpa opened his eyes and said, "Tracy, Andre, I need to change into a gown now. Would you two mind going to the patient library on the fifth floor? There's a packet of information waiting for me."

"Sure," I said.

"No problem," Andre grinned. We stood up. "Come on, Tracy." He put his hand on my arm as we headed for the elevator. Was he trying to be friends? Did he think everything was the same as before? I thought of Toni's matching fingernails, lipstick, and hair. I stepped away from his hand and into the elevator.

Inside the patient library, the cancer resource nurse, a woman about fifty with graying brown hair, smiled hugely when we explained that we were picking up a packet for Bart Andrew.

"I'm Terri," she said, holding out her hand. I noticed that she had a thin white scar sliding down the left side of her cheek, like a trail left over from a tear. "Are you Bart's grandchildren?" she asked as she led us through the library into her back office.

"Yes," Andre said before I had a chance to reply. I didn't contradict him. If he wanted to claim Grandpa, that was OK. It would make us cousins and solve some problems.

Then I noticed two plaques on Terri's desk. One said: "Don't hesitate to ask questions! Knowledge is power." The other said: "Today is life. Live today well!"

Terri cheerfully handed me a manila envelope stuffed with papers. "This is a packet for the families of our advanced cancer patients," she explained. "It even contains a picture book explaining the disease to children. It will tell you what to expect during the next two months and teach you how other families have coped. We find that families need to know the truth and have as much information as possible. The truth is more comforting and easier to deal with than the unknown."

"Thanks," I said.

We left the library and waited for the elevator.

Suddenly, Andre turned to me. His eyes smoldered and his voice was toneless as he said, "How can the truth be comforting when it's about Bart's suffering and death?"

"You have a point," I said dismally. We rode the elevator in silence.

A few minutes later, we were back with Grandpa. He wore a pale blue hospital gown.

"How's my boyfriend?" A short Hispanic woman in a white coat flounced into the room and put her arm around Grandpa.

"Gloria." Grandpa turned towards Andre and me. "I want you to meet Tracy and Andre."

Gloria pumped our hands, exuding energy. "Tracy and

Andre, I'm not really your grandpa's girl; I'm his radiation therapist. Come on, I'll introduce you to the machine."

In the treatment room, Gloria showed us how the laser lights targeted the area being radiated. She showed off the linear accelerator, moving it up, down, and around. Andre asked a bunch of questions about gamma rays and tangents. Gloria was impressed.

After answering Andre's questions, Gloria whipped out ten neon-colored magic markers, explaining to Andre that she used those to mark the skin in the treated area. "Bart, honey," she said as she gently rubbed Grandpa's arm, "which color do you want today?"

Andre and I went out into the hall when Grandpa climbed onto the table. Gloria finished setting the machine. Seconds later, she came out and closed the thick lead doors. She turned on a monitor so that she could watch Grandpa during his treatment.

I felt like I was in an episode of the *X-Files* as I focused on the small screen. The still, human figure on the table contained the soul of my grandfather. I wanted so badly to feel Andre's arm around me, to lean into him, to be comforted. But lead doors aren't the only things that separate people from each other.

On the way home, Grandpa told us about a dream he'd had a few nights before. "There was a barrier directly in front of me," he said, "like a blanket or fog of blackness. A voice told me to reach through the darkness. I stretched out my hand, and the darkness evaporated into a world of light. It was a nice dream."

"It sounds nice," I said, and I took Grandpa's hand. Andre sat in the backseat, absolutely silent.

Chapter 13

LIES

That evening, during dinner, Mom announced that we were going to go around the table and compliment each other. Rob and I moaned.

"Come on," Mom cajoled, "I heard about this in Relief Society. It's supposed to make the family closer. Besides, no compliment, no dessert."

"This is coercion," Rob said, "but, if it'll make Mom happy, I'll start. I want to compliment Katie for biting the dental assistant rather than the dentist."

I giggled. Mom eyed Rob disapprovingly. "You must not be very hungry, son." She turned to Katie and continued, "I want to compliment Katie for being so brave when the dentist gave her a shot!" (Mom believed in ignoring bad behavior and praising good. Maybe that was why Rob was immature and Katie was out of control.)

"Katie's turn now," Mom said sweetly. Katie surveyed us like she was the queen and we were slime beneath her feet. "I want to compliment Casey for writing me a letter," she said primly.

"No dessert for you!" Rob exclaimed, thumping his hand on his knee. "You're supposed to compliment someone here."

"Mom just said it had to be someone in our family," Katie

retorted, "and Casey *is* in our family!" Katie stuck her tongue out at Rob. In return, Rob pushed up her chin, causing her to bite her tongue. Katie shrieked in pain and kicked Rob hard. Rob was about to retaliate, when Mom screamed, "Stop this!" Her voice was high and shrill, completely out of character. Katie stopped yelling, and Rob looked down at his plate.

I thought Mom was going to cry, but she took a deep breath and composed herself. "Tracy," she said, "it's your turn." I was about to forego dessert by saying that I wasn't in the mood, when I looked at Dad. He looked tired.

"I want to compliment Dad for being such an awesome science teacher," I said, "and such a great dad."

Dad took off his glasses and pulled a handkerchief out of his pocket. He dabbed at his eyes.

"John, it's your turn," Mom reminded him.

Dad looked around the table. Rob shoveled down a mouthful of food. Katie piled butter onto her mashed potato castle. Mom looked at Dad expectantly.

"I want to compliment all of you," Dad said, "for being so supportive. You are my greatest blessings." We all stared at Dad. There wasn't a hint of sarcasm in his voice. I wondered what had caused him to lose touch with reality.

Later that evening I found out. I was in my room, sitting at my desk, drowning in homework. Dad opened the door.

"Tracer," he said, "I thought you might want to know what happened at the faculty meeting today."

I swiveled around in my chair. "What?" I asked.

Dad sat down on my bed and began, "Mr. Littlejon introduced two new teachers who will be starting in January. One's the new basketball coach, a guy named Michael J. Hamilton, Michael *Jordan* Hamilton."

I cracked up. Dad continued, "The other guy's a science teacher fresh out of college with a master's degree. He'll be taking over my AP Physics and Advanced Chemistry courses."

"You're not serious."

Dad nodded. I knew that Dad had an incredibly heavy teaching load and that the administration had been looking for a new teacher to help out. But this left Dad with Freshman Science and Beginning Chemistry. Dad loved his advanced courses. Cunningham and Littlejon knew that.

"I can't believe it!" I burst. "Cunningham's getting you back for disagreeing with him!"

"I talked to Brad about it briefly after the meeting. He told me that he's a lame duck now, that it's Elvin's decision." Dad's shoulders slumped. I walked over and sat down by him on the bed. He continued, "Honey, I haven't told your mom or grandfather. I feel like a failure."

"Dad, you're not a failure. You're an awesome teacher! You're an awesome person!" I said passionately. I hated seeing Dad spent and beaten. I hated the people who were doing this to him. "The bishop shouldn't have asked you to speak at the school board meeting," I said heavily.

"I don't regret that, Tracy." Dad straightened up. "Long ago, I made a lifetime decision to live a certain way."

"I think you should fight the administration," I said.

"I've decided to wait," Dad went on. "I'm going to help your grandfather through his ordeal. Then I'll think about leaving Haltsburg."

I rubbed Dad's shoulders. I knew how it felt to have things go wrong, to feel helpless.

On Friday, the sun shone brightly, and the temperature rose throughout the day. The weather had changed from unseasonably stormy to unseasonably warm.

During last-period announcements, Mrs. Hattinger, Mr. Littlejon's secretary, read the names of the new homecoming court over the intercom. I cheered out loud when she announced Kallie as one of the princesses. Mrs. Hattinger said that each member of the court would pick her own escort. I thought of how Kal would look elegant on the homecoming royalty float, in her tapering red silk dress set off with ebony beads and tall, dark Marcus by her side. Perhaps it would make homecoming bearable.

The bell rang. I hurried to our locker to congratulate Kallie. When I got there, Tricia Otto, who helped in the office during third period, blocked my way. She grabbed my arm and whispered, "I need to talk to you before Kallie comes! Kallie was made princess because she's black!"

I glared at Tricia. I had always liked Tricia. Until now.

"It's not because she's black!" I hissed. "It's because she's wonderful. The student body couldn't have made a better choice."

"I like Kallie too," Tricia explained. "But the student body didn't choose her. When I was working in the office this morning, I overheard the administrators talking. Kallie didn't have enough votes. Cunningham included Kallie for political reasons. He wants Haltsburg High to be progressive and politically correct."

"Why are you telling me this? Do you have any idea how hurt Kallie would be if she knew?"

"I'm telling you because you're Kallie's best friend. If word gets out, I thought you should know the truth."

"Maybe I don't want to know the truth," I said. I suddenly remembered the poem from Ms. Hahn's class, the poem about the knife blades on the pathway to truth.

"Poor Kallie!" I exclaimed with venom. I hated the school administration for what they did to my dad, for what they were doing to Kallie. Tricia disappeared without another word.

An instant later I knew why. I felt strong hands on my shoulders. I turned around. Marcus looked into my eyes. "Why poor Kallie?" he asked. I held his gaze for a moment. I hated lies! I was sick of lies. Maybe the truth hurt, but a lie . . . a lie was like cancer. I blurted out everything Tricia had told me, halfway hoping Marcus would splinter the facade by rearranging Cunningham's face.

Marcus was quiet for a long moment, then he made a decision. “I’m not going to tell Kallie,” he said. “I don’t want her knowing she’s been disrespected. She’s the only African-American in a class full of whites. She deserves to be a princess. I’m asking you not to tell her either.”

I felt my shoulders sag. I wasn’t good at lies. “OK,” I said miserably.

“Tracy,” he added. “I’ll wear a smile on that float. You’ll act cheerful and dance with Brice. You and I, we’ll act like we’re enjoying homecoming even if it kills us.”

“It might kill us,” I said. “Our survival is definitely in jeopardy.” Marcus grinned at me. He put his arm around my shoulder. I felt as if a great weight were lifted from me.

Later that afternoon, I thought about a quote Mom had tacked on the fridge. It compared the slow forming of a friendship to a cup filled one drop at a time. At last there comes a moment when a drop fills the cup, and it begins to run over. It’s like that with friendship. You share moments with another person, like drops of water in the cup. Then you suddenly realize that the person has become your friend, that the cup is full. Now Marcus was my friend.

Chapter 14

I AM

Halloween arrived on a Tuesday. Rob and I went to a youth activity at Brother Reynold's barn. I wore jeans and an orange T-shirt that said "Chill out! THIS is my costume!"

As soon as we got there, Rob, who was dressed like one of the Beatles, ran to find his other Beatle friends. I paused at the door, surveying the pumpkins, streamers, and the motley collection of characters. Then I spotted Kallie in the corner by a steaming kettle of dry ice. Marcus was with her. I weaved my way towards them.

"Hey, Kal," I said as I approached, "great costume!" She wore a black column dress, black fishnet stockings, chunky black heels, and a witch's hat.

"Trace, this is *not* a costume!" she said, fingering my sleeve. I thought about the year before, when Andre, Kallie, and I came as the *Star Trek* crew.

"I wasn't in the mood," I sighed. "Besides, Marcus isn't dressed up either."

Kallie took a black headband with attached cat ears out of her purse. She reached up and put them on Marcus. "He's my black cat!" she teased, hugging him.

"Sure." Marcus pulled the cat ears off and smiled into Kallie's eyes.

While Marcus and Kallie exchanged intimate looks, Brice

appeared beside me, dressed like a missionary in a dark gray suit. He even had an official-looking name tag.

"What do you think?" he asked, throwing out his arms as if he were on display.

"Authentic," I said.

"I'm wearing this Saturday night," he added, "minus the name tag. What color is your dress?"

"Jade," I answered, thinking about the linen dress I had picked out the previous weekend. It had shoulder pads, a wide waistband, and a fitted skirt that hit just above my knees. The classic look.

A moment later, Rob and the rest of the Beatles gathered around us. Brice did the electric slide in time with his newest tongue twister, "The blue-black bug bled blue-black blood on the bare barn floor." Kallie and Marcus laughed. As the Beatles chimed in, I sighed and wondered if I'd be able to survive homecoming weekend.

On Friday night at the homecoming game, the stadium lights glared under a purple-black sky. I sat in the center of the bleachers with Dad, Rob, and Katie. Marcus and Kallie were behind us with Kallie's mom and Danika. In another section, I spotted Andre and Toni with Grant and Anita. Andre had his arm around Toni.

While Sandy Medio, a junior, sang the national anthem a cloud blew over the three-quarter moon, glowing with light. It reminded me of the ocean at night—the way the full moon tenderly illuminates the inside of a growing wave, until it breaks.

Gazing at the sky caused me to think about Grandpa. Every day, he seemed more and more like a shining spirit in a fading body. I thought of how the doctor had stopped Grandpa's radiation therapy earlier in the week. The treatments couldn't help him anymore. The hospice nurse brought oxygen to our home that day. Soon the body would break and Grandpa's spirit would be gone.

The announcer yelled, "Play ball!" Cheers shook the bleachers. I spotted Brice looking lost at the bottom of the stands as the cheerleaders screamed, "Don't forget! We're the best. We're much better than all the rest!" Brice searched the crowd for someone to sit by.

Kallie came to his rescue. During the instant of silence following the kick off, while the ball sailed through the air, she whistled to Brice. He climbed straight up through the packed bleachers, ignoring the dirty looks he received, and squeezed in between Danika and Sidney, directly behind me.

By the end of the first quarter, Haltsburg was up thirteen zip. Marcus and Kallie left to change into formal clothes for the halftime ceremony. Robbie bought a hot dog. When Dad wasn't watching, Robbie said, "Look, magic!" Then, in about 3 seconds, he literally sucked the hot dog down! It shocked me so much that I choked on my nachos. Brice pounded my back and offered to do mouth to mouth.

During halftime, the floats carrying the homecoming court rounded the football field before parking on the fifty yard line. The homecoming king and escorts helped the queen and princesses down.

The homecoming king and queen were introduced. Then the intercom blared out the name of Kallie Thompson, the senior princess, and her escort, Marcus Smith. We stood up and screamed and whistled until our throats ached. I noticed that Andre and Toni were screaming and whistling too. Lights flashed as a photographer took pictures.

Saturday morning, I saw the pictures on the front page of the *Haltsburg Herald.* The other princesses smiled, but Kallie beamed. Marcus stood next to her with his pasted smile, as protective and silent as the Secret Service.

That night, before the dance, Brice picked me up in his cousin's Firebird. We nabbed Kallie and headed over to Montagues' to get Marcus. On the way, we passed Andre in his Toyota. I knew he was on his way to get Toni. I silently wished that I could slip through a worm hole into another universe—a universe where Andre and I were together.

We arrived at the Rancher's for dinner. As we trailed the hostess to our table, Brice took my hand. I made sure my fingers went as limp as spaghetti. During dinner, I thanked Marcus when he convinced Brice that a bean-eating contest would *not* be cool. Before leaving for the dance, Kallie and I made a stop at the rest room.

"Trace," she said as I brushed my hair, "are you having any fun?"

I focused on the corsage of pink roses on my wrist. "The prime rib was good," I said, not wanting to spoil her evening. "How 'bout you?"

"I'm a homecoming princess on a date with the guy I love. Plus, next Saturday is my baptism. My dreams are coming true," Kallie said simply.

"I'm glad." I forced myself to smile at her, knowing full well that it wasn't real.

"There's just one thing wrong," Kallie said as she put her arm around me. "I'm worried about my best friend."

"I'm fine," I lied as I brushed blush on my cheeks and braced myself for the rest of the evening.

At the dance, Toni wore a sexy, shell-colored dress with the back cut out. Her red hair was piled high. Andre looked great in his light gray suit. I forced myself to stop staring at them. Every once in a while, I felt as if Andre's eyes were on me. But each time I looked at him, he was immersed in Toni. The evening wore on as I endured Brice's tongue-twisting, movie-trivia chatter.

Finally, there was only a half hour of agony left. I danced stiffly with Brice during the song "Lady in Red." I watched Andre and Toni sway together. Marcus held Kallie close.

"*I am!*" Brice's voice in my ear suddenly broke into my thoughts.

"From the *Ten Commandments*," I responded. Brice had been throwing around movie trivia all evening.

"No!" Brice hissed, his voice louder than a whisper. "*I am!* A form of the verb—*to be!* From the *Life of Brice Miller. I am! I am* here! *I am* your date! I exist even if you don't see me!"

"Shh, Brice," I whispered, feeling panicky. I didn't want people listening. Why had I ever agreed to go out with him? "I see you!" I said. "I'm dancing with you!"

"No you're not!" Brice stopped in the middle of the floor. We stood in dance position, our feet frozen. "You're letting me dance with you! All *you* see is Andre Sousa! You're not dancing with me!"

I heard the frustration in his voice and knew the truth of his words. But what was I supposed to do? Pretend something I didn't feel? It was totally embarrassing standing stone still while couples danced around us, eyeing us like we were idiots. Then Toni spotted us. With her arms around Andre's neck she reached up on her tiptoes and whispered something in his ear.

"Forget Andre Sousa," I said, looking into Brice's pale blue-gray eyes. "Let's dance together!"

"Now that I have your attention," Brice said seriously, "I'm going to sweep you off your feet." The next song had a beat. Brice pulled me close. His feet were light, and he knew how to lead. Before I knew it, we were tearing up the dance floor with my long hair flying behind me, trying to catch up.

"Big bad Brice and a beautiful breathless babe burn rubber," Brice yelled as I twirled. I knew Andre was watching. Once I had wondered what it felt like to shed inhibitions and shine! Now I knew. It was scary and thrilling at the same time. I couldn't believe I was enjoying this. I laughed at myself.

"What's so funny?" Brice asked.

"Nobody's ever called me a 'beautiful breathless babe' before," I answered.

After the dance, Brice took me home. He draped his arm

around my shoulders as he walked me to the door. Please don't let him try to kiss me, I prayed.

Once we were on the front porch, I lightly punched Brice's shoulder. "Friends forever," I said.

"Funny funky friends forever!" Brice returned.

"I can do that too," I said lightly. "Frenzied fumbling funny funky friends forever!"

"Fabulous flirtatious frenzied fumbling funny funky friends forever!" Brice shot back.

"You win!" I reached for the doorknob.

"Tracy," Brice's voice stopped me before I went in. "Will you write me on my mission? I'll be finished with high school graduation requirements this semester. My papers are already in. I'm going to try to be a decent missionary."

I looked at Brice carefully. For the first time I saw something more. He was a lousy student, but he wasn't stupid. I had never been especially nice to him, but he wanted me to write to him. His mom and dad constantly criticized him, but he would try to be a good missionary.

The Brice I knew was crazy and outrageous. But I suddenly realized something. He was lonely too. With his neon hair and stupid comments, he had been working double time to get someone to notice him. "I exist," he had told me that night. "I, Brice Miller, exist."

I smiled at Brice. "Sure, I'll write you. What are friends for anyway?" Then I kissed his cheek before going into the house.

Chapter 15

Knowledge Is Power

Monday night was family night. Mom called for everyone to gather around the kitchen table. We usually had family home evening in the living room, but now the hospital bed had taken the sofa's place, and Grandpa needed his rest.

I noticed that there was dried food on the kitchen table. Rob and Katie had had kitchen duty, and they had done a lousy job. They'd been fighting instead of cleaning.

"Stop teasing me!" Katie continued the feud as she kicked Rob under the table. Rob grabbed her ankle and laughed. Furious, Katie tried to kick him with her other foot but hit my ankle instead. I yelped in pain and begged them to stop. Mom sat down and ran her fingers through her hair. She looked tired. I thought of the easel in her room holding the unfinished oceanscape. Mom hadn't painted since Grandpa moved in.

While Katie continued to fume, Dad asked Rob to say an opening prayer. Afterwards Dad took some papers out of a large manila envelope. I recognized the envelope. It was the one I brought home from the cancer center.

Dad shuffled the papers until he found his place. Then he cleared his throat, adjusted his glasses, and read aloud, "Knowledge is power because it educates us. This education increases our understanding and wisdom, our ability to live each day well. It helps us make choices."

Katie and Rob made faces at each other. Dad went on in his teacher's voice, "As a family we are very lucky to have knowledge. We know the gospel is true. We know Jesus was resurrected. We know we can be together forever as a family. We know that Grandpa will soon leave us and join Grandma.

"Mom and I talked to Grandpa's doctor yesterday. She said that Grandpa will die within the next two weeks. Mom and I wondered whether we should tell you children the timetable. But after we read that quote we decided it was something you deserved to know."

At this point, Mom interrupted, "Grandpa isn't in much pain now, and his mind is still clear. That is a great blessing from Heavenly Father. Talk to your grandpa. Tell him you love him. Tell him good-bye."

I felt an ache in my throat as Katie burst into song, "Families can be together forever through Heavenly Father's plan!"

"Shut up, stupid!" Rob said.

"Mommy, Rob called me stupid!" Katie shrieked as she kicked his shin.

I couldn't believe that they would fight at a time like this. I grabbed the manila envelope and slapped it against the table. "This is family night, not family fight!" I yelled.

Mom and Dad exchanged looks—the resident psychologists analyzing their offspring. Then Mom said with strained cheerfulness, "Now it's time for treats and the game."

I left the table and went into my room. I opened the novel we were reading in AP English and buried myself in the story.

That night, my dream came in reds and blacks. Grandpa was locked inside a burning one-room schoolhouse. I pounded on the door. Rain poured down, dousing the flames. Then the blackened door of the schoolhouse flew open. Grandpa stumbled out, his body covered with red sores. The rain washed his hurts away. He took my hand and we flew together, soaring above the clouds to where the sun shone.

Andre suddenly appeared in my dream, flying beside us, holding my hand. "Tracy and Bart," he said, looking directly at the sun, "did you know this star is made of an atomic blend of hydrogen, oxygen, and nitrogen? It will burn out someday."

Then Andre's hand grew hot in mine. The scorching increased, and I let go. He fell. Suddenly I was falling too, tumbling after him. Before I hit the ground, I jerked awake.

The next afternoon, I went directly from school to the Montagues'. I saddled Gozo and rode him hard. We did figure eights, working on lead changes. I was almost ready to give up when Gozo loped smoothly through the figure eight, attentive to my leg signals. Again and again he did it! I thought about how it sometimes takes a lot of practice to get something right.

After cooling him down, I slipped from the saddle and threw my arms around Gozo's neck. "I'm so proud of you, buddy!" I whispered in his ear. "So, so proud of you!"

Then I mucked out stalls and groomed the rest of the horses. I was just finishing up when Andre and Marcus pulled into the driveway. They were getting home from play practice.

"Hey," I said as I walked up to them both. I needed to talk to Andre. I needed to tell him that Grandpa's time was short.

"Hey, Tracy," Marcus said back, smiling broadly. Andre nodded, "Hi."

"How's rehearsal going?" I asked.

"It would be OK if Hahn wasn't a slave driver," Marcus laughed. Marcus and I talked about the play for another couple of minutes, but Andre remained quiet. Then he said he had homework to do and turned to go into the big house.

"Andre, wait," I said. "I need to talk to you." He turned his head, and his eyes met mine.

"I'll see you guys later. Gotta study these lines," Marcus added before ducking into the guest house.

"What's up?" Andre asked as I pulled myself into a sitting position on a nearby fence. Andre shifted himself up onto the fence next to me. I looked into the sky as I explained, "It's about Grandpa. The hospice nurse said he won't be here much longer. No more than two weeks. Probably less. I don't want you to stay away from Grandpa because of me, because things are different between us."

"I guess he won't be here for *The Winter's Tale,*" Andre said, looking down at his shoes.

"No," I said. "Even if he's still alive, he'll be too weak. I'm sorry." *The Winter's Tale* was three weeks away. I thought about how hard it would be for *me* to go to the play. We had practiced the lines with Grandpa. Yet Grandpa would be gone, and Toni would be onstage with Andre.

"Trace?" Andre's voice sounded thin, like he didn't have enough air. He continued, "When can I come over to see Bart?"

"Whenever you want," I said.

"OK."

There was nothing else to say. I lowered myself from the fence. As I walked to the car, I knew Andre wasn't thinking about Toni right then. But he wasn't thinking about me either. He was thinking about Grandpa.

Chapter 16

THE LIE SHATTERS

On Wednesday night, at our Laurel activity, we learned to make piecrusts. Sister Carlin demonstrated how to flute the edges. When she finished, she added, "This is only an example. Be creative and finish your pie shell any way you wish."

Kallie and I were the only Laurels who strayed from the norm. I rolled out my crust and put it in the pan. I left the edges hanging—the free, artsy look. Kallie worked carefully on her pie, weaving bits of crust in and out. When she finished, the border of her crust looked like the woven edge of a basket.

After the crusts baked and cooled, we heaped chocolate pudding into them. Then we sat down at tables in the cultural hall and ate our creations. I cut two pieces from my pie and handed one to Kallie since she was saving hers for Marcus. While I dug in, Sister Carlin pulled up a folding chair and sat down next to me, across from Kallie.

"Kallie, I love the edge of your pie. Where did you learn to do that?"

"My mom taught me. She loves to bake," Kallie grinned.

"Congratulations on your upcoming baptism." Sister Carlin's gray eyes made crinkle lines in her round face as she smiled at Kallie. Sister Carlin was *into* missionary work, partly because she and her husband had recently returned from a mission to Portugal.

"I'm excited," Kallie beamed. "By the way, Sister Carlin, there's something I need to ask you. Would you mind being one of the speakers?"

"I'd love to!" Sister Carlin's smile broadened. Her gray hair had silver highlights under the cultural hall lights. "Kallie, what would you like me to speak about?"

"Baptism," Kallie responded. Then she turned to me. "Tracy, would you give the other talk—on the Holy Ghost?"

I choked, splattering chocolate pudding on the white paper tablecloth. "Kal," I exclaimed, "thanks for the advance warning!"

Kallie laughed and dabbed at the pudding on the table with her napkin. "I'm sorry, Trace," she said. "Just yesterday the elders told me that I get to *pick* the speakers! You'll do it, won't you?"

"What are friends for?" I shrugged helplessly.

Then Sister Carlin stood up and laid her hand on Kallie's shoulder. "Dear," she said, "when we were on our mission, occasionally investigators had concerns right before their baptisms. I remember one brother whose aunt gave him confusing anti-Mormon literature. Another sister broke her arm and needed help wrapping the cast in plastic. Feel free to call me if you need to talk."

"I will, Sister Carlin," Kallie grinned. "But I don't think anything will come up. I'm betting on smooth sailing." Kallie couldn't have been more wrong.

It started during Government class. Mr. Jensen had been absent on Wednesday, so during the first ten minutes of class, he read the results of the class's mock election which had been held on Tuesday. Proposition 209, the proposal to stop affirmative action, won with 26 votes in favor and 2 against.

During lunch, the weather was nice so Kallie, Marcus, and I sprawled out on the grass to eat. Brice strolled up. Marcus squinted up at him and said seriously, "Bro, I thought you were against 209?"

"I am, my friend," Brice returned. "There were two votes against the proposition, yours and mine."

Marcus's eyes widened, and he turned his head. His gaze fell on Kallie. Her color deepened as she swallowed a bite from her apple. I realized that Marcus and I, two of the people closest to her, had assumed the same thing—that Kallie was against 209. We had assumed it because she was black. But Brice hadn't assumed anything. Maybe he was the only one of us who truly had no prejudice.

Brice broke the silence. "So . . . what's everybody having for lunch today?"

No one answered. Kallie put her hand on Marcus's arm and explained, "I'm in favor of 209. I don't think affirmative action is fair."

"It's a free country," Marcus said. But his voice was cold. A few minutes later, he said he had some stuff to do and walked away from us without looking back.

That afternoon, Kallie called me. "Trace," she begged, "will you go with me to see Marcus? He wouldn't speak to me during rehearsal! I've got to talk to him!"

"I'll pick you up in ten minutes," I said. "I need to clean stalls anyway."

When we arrived at Montagues', Marcus's truck was gone. Kallie helped me muck out Capricorn's stall. While we shoveled manure, she sang a Garth Brooks song. Kallie had always loved country music. As she sang this time I couldn't help but notice the words:

When the last thing we notice is the color of skin
And the first thing we look for is the beauty within
When the skies and the oceans are clean again
Then we shall be free

We shall be free
We shall be free
Stand straight, walk proud
'Cause we shall be free

A few minutes later, we heard Marcus's truck pull in. Kallie grabbed my hand. "Come with me, Trace." She sounded scared.

I went outside with Kallie. She ran up to Marcus as he climbed out of his truck. He tried to walk past her. She grabbed both of his hands and made him look at her.

"Marcus, talk to me," she begged. "I love you."

"You let me down," he said flatly.

"Can't I be proud of being black and in favor of 209?" Kallie asked.

"No," Marcus said simply. "The two don't go together. You're an Oreo."

I heard a strange half sob rise from Kallie. Right then I didn't know why Marcus's comment hurt so much. Later I found out. An Oreo is black on the outside and white on the inside.

When Kallie spoke again, she was pleading. "It's just that I don't want a break because of my color! I don't want to get into college because I'm black. I don't want a job because a quota needs to be filled. I want people to look at who I am and what I've done! I want them to see me!"

Marcus suddenly looked very tired. "Kallie," he said as if he were explaining something to a child, "you *are* your color. Why do you think you were chosen to be a homecoming princess? You didn't have enough votes. The administration did it because you're black."

"You're lying!" Kallie exclaimed.

"I don't lie," Marcus said. "Ask Tracy!" Then he turned and went into the guest house.

Kallie whirled towards me.

“Oh, Kal!” I said, reaching out to her feebly. “I didn’t tell you because I didn’t want you to be hurt! Please don’t hate me!”

“I don’t hate you,” Kallie whispered with her hands clenched and tears streaming down her cheeks. “Just take me home.”

While I drove Kallie home I wanted to put my arm around her, to say something to make things better, maybe joke about all the trouble ADD and PMS had caused us. But when I looked at her sitting silently with her arms folded and mascara stains on her cheeks, I knew she didn’t want me to touch her.

I turned a corner sharply, hating Marcus for hurting her. But it was my fault too. I had known something and not told her. I had become part of the lie. By doing that, I had let her color separate us. I didn’t see her for who she was—the confident, beautiful girl who could splinter the facade. Instead, I became part of the system that betrayed her.

Chapter 17

The Tree of Righteousness

That night, I couldn't sleep. The year before, I had read in a novel that there are no happy endings. If someone is happy then it means the end hasn't come yet. I had laughed when I read that, knowing it wasn't true. But that night I wasn't so sure. Just twenty-four hours ago, Kallie had been so happy. Just a few months ago, I had Kallie and Andre, the two best friends in the universe.

An hour later, I looked at my clock. It was 1:30 in the morning. My head ached. I went into the kitchen to get a drink of milk and take some Tylenol. How would I be able to wake up in four hours for seminary? At least it was Friday. I only had to get through the day.

I poured myself some milk and sat down at the kitchen table. My thoughts wove on. Saturday was Kallie's baptism. Was she OK? I needed to prepare my talk. Would Kallie ever forgive me?

I rested my head in my hands. Then I heard a voice from the living room. In the still night, Grandpa's hoarse whisper was very clear. "Tracy, is that you?"

"Yes, Grandpa."

"Can't sleep?" he asked.

"No." I went into the living room and sat in a chair next to Grandpa's bed. I took his hand. His fingers were so thin that they didn't look short and chunky anymore, just fragile and wrinkled.

"I'm not sleepy either," he said. I thought about how I used to tell Grandpa everything. But the past week I'd been keeping my problems to myself. Was it because I didn't want to burden him with the details of my life? Or was it because I was practicing living without him?

"Andre hasn't stopped by lately," Grandpa commented. "I miss him."

"He'll come by soon," I offered. "He wants to see you. I think he's been staying away because of me. Because we aren't close anymore."

"I'm sorry," Grandpa said. I thought of Toni and the R-rated movie controversy—the things that pushed us apart. But the wedge had already been there. The wedge had something to do with Andre's passion to understand everything from the human body to the universe. Yet he couldn't understand or accept the existence of God.

"Honey," Grandpa said a moment later, "could you flip on the lamp and hand me my scriptures. There are some things I've been wanting to share with you." Then he added with a soft chuckle, "Remember the last time we talked this late at night?"

I nodded and thought of a night over two years before when I stayed with Grandpa in the schoolhouse. I had just found out about his heart condition. We had looked at the stars together and Grandpa had explained how the gospel and the stars gave him hope.

I turned on the lamp and retrieved Grandpa's scriptures from the coffee table. The print was large, and there were lots of colored tabs marking his favorite passages. I handed

Grandpa his reading glasses and tilted his hospital bed into a sitting position. The house was very quiet except for the ticking of the clock and the whir of an occasional car out on the road. Angel lay curled up at the foot of Grandpa's bed.

"Tracy," he said, "right now Andre is asking the 'how' questions. How did the world evolve? How can we cure cancer? Someday things might change. Andre might start asking 'why.' Why does the universe exist? Why is suffering a part of our lives? There aren't any easy answers, but there are some scriptures that have helped me. If I don't have time to share this with Andre, would you?"

"I'll try," I said.

"The first scripture is about truth. It's from the Doctrine and Covenants, section ninety-three." Grandpa turned clumsily to a green tab and read. " 'And truth is knowledge of things as they are, and as they were, and as they are to come. . . . All truth is independent in that sphere in which God has placed it, to act for itself, as all intelligence also; otherwise there is no existence.' "

Grandpa continued, "The next scripture is from the book of Moses. Moses asks, 'Why are these things so?' The Lord tells Moses, 'This is my work and my glory—to bring to pass the immortality and eternal life of man.'"

Grandpa took a raspy breath. I knew he was tired. "Tracy, there isn't much time," he said weakly.

"I know," I whispered as I took his hand.

"There's one more scripture I want to show you. It's about the Savior's mission and about trees."

Grandpa and I shared this love for trees. He had taken me to see the giant redwoods. He had taught me about liquidambar, crape myrtle, and eucalyptus.

"It's Isaiah talking about the Messiah," Grandpa whispered. "It's what I want for you." Then Grandpa spoke without opening his scriptures. His voice wasn't weak as he quoted, " 'Give unto them beauty for ashes, the oil of joy for mourning, the garment of praise for the spirit of heaviness; that they might be called trees of righteousness, the planting of the Lord, that he might be glorified.' "

As Grandpa spoke, I thought of Kallie, and tears jumped to my eyes. I hoped that Heavenly Father, through Jesus, would dry her tears and change them to joy. I hoped he would do that for all of us.

Grandpa rested his head on the pillow. His moustache now looked oversized in contrast with his gaunt, chiseled features. I lowered his bed, took his scriptures, folded his glasses, and slipped them into their case.

"I'm going to miss you, Grandpa," I said. "I love you."

"I'll always be with you," Grandpa said. "We're sealed together. Every talk that we've had, everything I am, will always be a part of you. You are the planting of the Lord."

I kissed Grandpa's cheek, remembering how it used to feel leathery from the wind and sun. Now, it felt dry and parched, like an autumn leaf. "And you are the tree of righteousness," I whispered.

Chapter 18

SEQUENCE OF EVENTS

On Friday morning, Kallie didn't show up for seminary. Before first period, I waited at our locker until the late bell rang. Then I gave up and went to class.

During AP English, Toni leaned over and put her head on Andre's shoulder. Would I ever get a grip and quit noticing everything they did? Then Ms. Hahn passed out a poem called "Words" by Sylvia Plath. It went like this:

> Axes
> After whose stroke the wood rings,
> And the echoes!
> Echoes travelling
> Off from the centre like horses.
>
> The sap
> Wells like tears, like the
> Water striving
> To re-establish its mirror
> Over the rock
>
> That drops and turns,
> A white skull,
> Eaten by weedy greens.

Years later I
Encounter them on the road—

Words dry and riderless
The indefatigable hoof-taps.
While
From the bottom of the pool, fixed stars
Govern a life.

"The author, Sylvia Plath, was thirty when she died," Ms. Hahn said loudly. "People, what is she saying in this poem?"

Nobody raised a hand. Ms. Hahn paced back and forth, her eyes flashing. She was definitely in a bad mood.

Then she pointed to John Corathers, who stretched lazily in his chair. "John, I want some ideas."

"Well . . . ," John yawned, "maybe the author, Sylvia what's-her-name, was, like, walking through the woods when she found the skull of someone who had been murdered by an ax. Maybe the author was, like, the ax murderer. Hey! She could have, like, gone to prison and written the poem before her execution."

"Right," Ms. Hahn snorted, totally unamused by John's interpretation. "People, think!" she practically yelled. "I've taught you about metaphors! I've taught you about allegories. I've taught you about similes. This poem is symbolic! The title is 'Words' not 'Murder One.' Think about it!"

Ms. Hahn sat down on her stool and folded her arms, glaring at us. The only sound in the room was Ms. Hahn's high heel tapping nervously on the floor. No one responded. The poem totally confused us.

After five minutes of silence, Ms. Hahn let out another disgusted snort. "If you people are going to pass the AP exam, you are going to have to learn to think for yourselves! As this discussion isn't getting us anywhere, I want you to spend the rest of the period studying the poem. Then write an essay on its symbols and theme. Essays are due on Monday."

The room was silent while Ms. Hahn stewed. A note circulated through the class. When it reached me, I noticed that it had been started by Doug Miaki, a computer nerd. "Everybody, meet me tonight in cyberspace! We'll dissect this stupid poem in a teen chat room!" He included his nickname and the channel.

Another person had written on the same paper, "Forget Doug! There's a party at Hattinglys' tonight!" Some unknown person had added, "Hahn's a witch today. Anybody know why?" Another anonymous comment: "Her monthly challenge!" Somebody else: "Very funny! You're warped!"

I had passed the note on without adding to it when Ms. Hahn's voice broke my thoughts. "Tracy Barton, stay after class. I want to talk to you." Was she mad at me for that stupid note? This wasn't like her.

After the bell rang, I lingered at my desk. Andre came and stood over me. I looked up at him.

"What did you do?" he asked lightly. I glanced at Toni waiting for Andre by the doorway. She smiled at me with daggers in her eyes.

I shrugged, looking back at him. "I haven't a clue." Then I added, "When are you going to come and see Grandpa? He asked about you."

"I have to work after school today and most of Saturday. How about Sunday? I could stay with Bart while you guys go to church." At that point, Toni sidled up to Andre and took his hand.

"Sunday would be OK," I said, completely ignoring Toni's presence. This was about Grandpa, and Toni was a nonentity. I wondered briefly if I should tell Andre not to wait until Sunday to see Grandpa, that every day counted.

Andre must have partially read my thoughts because he said, "Call me if Bart gets worse, and I'll be over. Anytime."

" 'Dre." Toni squeezed his hand and gazed into his eyes.

I was surprised to see Andre's jaw tighten. Toni was getting on his nerves, and she didn't know it. I knew Andre's moods and expressions better than she did.

"I don't want to be late for class," Toni continued. "I'll see you at lunch." She stretched up and kissed him. I stared at the ceiling and drummed my fingers on my desk.

After Toni was gone, I looked at Andre and motioned towards Hahn at her desk. "Now that the leech has left, you'll leave me to the lioness," I said.

Andre actually grinned at my alliteration. "Trace, don't worry about Hahn. She probably wants to compliment you on your last essay."

"Right," I said sarcastically. "She seems to be in a very complimentary mood."

Ms. Hahn jammed some papers in her desk drawer. "I'd better go," Andre said. "Later."

"Bye." I watched him walk away in blue jeans and a navy polo shirt. He was masculine and graceful at the same time. I sighed. Before Andre reached the door, Ms. Hahn swept over to me.

"Tracy," she said fiercely, "I heard this morning that your father's schedule is changing! Why is he giving up his advanced classes?"

For a moment, I stared at her, too shocked to say anything. Finally I got out, "You mean you don't know?"

"No, I don't know, and nobody's giving me any clear answers! When I asked your father, he told me that it was a long story. I'm not a patient person. This new teacher has no experience and only half his skill."

"But you're on their side!" I stuttered.

"No, I am absolutely *not* on their side, whoever 'they' are!" Ms. Hahn hissed as her next class trickled in. She dragged me into the outdoor hallway. Andre was there! His backpack was on the ground, and he was fiddling with one of the straps. There wasn't a trace of Toni. Did he purposely hang around? Had he heard our entire conversation?

Suddenly, I was sick and tired of all the lies! First Dad was hurt and now Kallie. Truth was knowledge of things as they were, as they are, and as they are to come. Ms. Hahn and Andre were part of the reason that Dad was hurt! They were part of the stupid R-rated movie controversy. I blurted out the truth, praying silently that Dad wouldn't mind, that I was doing the right thing.

"Cunningham tried to force Dad to be in favor of R-rated movies," I said bitterly while looking straight at Ms. Hahn. "He wanted a unified school. When Dad wouldn't give in, he threatened him. He said that there might be changes, that Dad doesn't have tenure. Then they took away Dad's favorite classes. You might not believe me, but it's the truth."

Ms. Hahn sucked in a deep breath and studied her pointed, maroon fingernails. "Tracy." She looked up into my eyes. "I believe you." I suddenly felt a rush of warmth and appreciation for Ms. Hahn. She treated her students as fully formed young adults rather than quasi-people.

Ms. Hahn continued, "What I'm going to say now I trust you won't repeat. Brad Littlejon was a decent administrator. But his mind's on retirement. Elvin Cunningham has the job wrapped up. But if he thinks he's going to run this school through coercion and manipulation, he has another think coming! I'm going to the office right now to confront him.

"Elvin can't afford to lose me," Ms. Hahn continued, smiling knowingly and cunningly. "I have one of the highest AP passing rates in the state and one of the biggest mouths."

I grappled with what Ms. Hahn had just said. She was going to bat for Dad, even though they were on opposite sides of the *R* controversy. What would the repercussions be? Would she be hurt too? What had I done?

"B-but, you have a class right now," I stammered.

"Andre Sousa!" Ms. Hahn wheeled around. Andre was *still* working on his backpack. "As you've been eavesdropping on this entire conversation, you can go in and teach my English Lit class. They read *The Winter's Tale* this week. You have the whole thing memorized, so you ought to be able to lead a discussion. Quote some lines to them. Be an actor! I'll get you excused from your next class."

"Sure thing," Andre replied dutifully.

"Ms. Hahn, don't you want to think about this first?" I suggested.

"No! I do better when I'm heated! I'm not going to wait around and dilute my emotion! If Elvin Cunningham thinks I'm going to support him just because I want to choose the movies I show . . . He's dipping his fingers into a person's life! He's trying to control a teacher's right to his or her own opinion! Intolerable!"

"Good luck," I said hesitantly.

Ms. Hahn took off down the hallway. Then Andre stuck his head out the door and yelled, "Go, girl!" I couldn't believe he did that. Hahn turned around and laughed like the Wicked Witch of the West.

"And while you're in the office," I called out, suddenly catching her spirit, "tell Mr. Cunningham that Kallie Thompson knows about the votes. He owes her an apology!"

Ms. Hahn turned and looked at me briefly with a confused expression. Then she grinned and nodded and called back, "Will do!"

Inside the room, Andre was talking to the class about Leontes's jealousy and the tragic sequence of events it triggered in the first half of the play. I leaned against the wall as the tardy bell rang. What sequence of events would my disclosure to Ms. Hahn trigger? I had messed up with Kallie by not telling the truth. Had I messed up now by telling the truth? Do the things you know guide your choices, or do they just complicate them?

Chapter 19

FALLING ALL THE TIME

The rest of the school day passed in a whirl. Kallie was late for Government. Once there, she chose a desk in the back of the room instead of taking the seat I'd saved for her. At lunch hour, there was a note on our locker. "Trace," it said, "don't wait for me. Danika came. We went out."

When I got home that afternoon, I still hadn't seen Kallie. I went into my room and threw my backpack on my desk. I wanted so much for things to be OK with Kallie, to see her smile and hear her laugh. Had she purposely avoided me? I dug the AP poem out of my notebook and tried working on the essay. I couldn't concentrate. Was Kallie OK? I picked up the phone on my desk and dialed her number. Danika answered.

"Hi," I said, "is Kallie there?"

"She won't be home from rehearsal until 4:30," Danika explained. Leticia screamed in the background. Was Danika's voice less friendly than usual, or was it just my imagination? "Want me to have her call you?" Danika asked curtly.

"Yeah, I need to go out to the barn right now. I should be back about the time Kallie gets home."

"If you see Marcus Smith, tell him where to go," Danika said coldly.

"I won't see him," I said. "He's at rehearsal too." The line was silent for a few seconds. Then Danika swore. I felt sick in the pit of my stomach. I chose my words carefully as tears stung my eyes, "Danika, I'm really sorry Kallie is hurt. I feel so bad."

"It's not your fault, Tracy," Danika said. "Marcus is the one who dissed my little sister."

When I arrived at the barn, I felt this intense yearning to ride Gozo until we both dropped. But I knew I needed to work first. Yesterday, I never got to Sagittarius's or Shamara's stalls. I haltered and led the horses into the paddock. Then I shoveled manure into a wheelbarrow. I thought about how I had no life. It's pretty pathetic when your Friday plans consist of shoveling muck and doing homework.

I took a load out. As I hoisted the wheelbarrow handles, I thought about how I'd never been super outgoing. It had been OK because I had the two best friends anywhere. But now both relationships were strained. I forcefully dumped the load into the manure pile. Before pushing the wheelbarrow back to the barn, I slipped off one of my work gloves and wiped my brow. Tonight I could always get on the Internet and discuss the poem with Doug Miaki. Or I could call Brice and get an enlightening lesson on alliteration, or take Rob and Katie to some stupid movie.

I put my glove back on and trudged into the barn. After I laid out fresh straw, I grabbed Gozo's halter and lead rope. I went out to the brim of the big pasture and called for him. He didn't come. I called again. Nothing.

I opened the gate and walked towards the first hill. I knew that as soon as I climbed to the top, I'd be able to see the entire pasture. As I walked, I thought about the day Gozo was born, two years before. Andre and I had watched the pretty mare, Shamara, bring him into the world. It was the first time I had witnessed a birth.

I pictured myself following Andre's instructions as we helped Shamara with the labor. After Gozo was born, Andre told me to hug him and blow in his eyes and ears. I did. It was a magical moment, a moment I'd never forget. Then Andre named the colt Gozo, which means "joy" in Portuguese.

We had laughed while Gozo tried to stand. The little horse kept falling. There was nothing we could do to help him. He had to stand on his own. After thirty-plus tries, he did it. Andre explained that a horse needs to be able to stand and run for survival, and a little one won't give up until he gets it.

The wind in my hair brought me back to the present. When I reached the top of the hill, I saw Gozo in the far corner of the field, rubbing his nose against the fence. I stood still for a minute, feeling the warm November sun on my face. I looked at the huge puddles of water left over from the recent storms and at the fields that were turning lime green for the winter.

Then Gozo tore through the pasture with his tail high. I thought of the wobbly foal who was gone forever. Now he could gallop. It was a miracle, and it was instinct. It was safety and survival.

Safety and survival are important to people too. And we're sort of like foals in another way. We fall all the time. And falling hurts. It can hurt so bad that some people give up or take drugs to lessen the pain. And sometimes people push each other down. The day before, Kallie had been pushed down. And the following day I was supposed to give a talk on the Holy Ghost at her baptism. I prayed silently that the Holy Ghost would guide Kallie now and help her to stand.

I called to Gozo. His finely cut Arabian ears pricked forward, and he frisked up to me. I put my arm under his neck and slipped the halter on. He tried to jerk away as I put it over his nose. I noticed two strange pricks near his right nostril.

I pulled an old rubbery carrot out of my jeans pocket, and Gozo took it from my flattened palm. I looked closely at his nose. The pricked area was tender and a bit swollen. "Oh, Gozo," I said, hugging him and smelling his warmth. "What have you been into this time?"

I was almost to the barn with Gozo when I noticed Marcus's truck in the driveway. I looked at my watch. It was only four. Had he come home from rehearsal early? A moment later, the front door of the guest house swung open and Marcus appeared. We briefly made eye contact. Then Marcus began walking quickly towards me.

I looked away and hurried Gozo into the barn. I didn't want to speak to Marcus! How could he face me after what he had done to Kallie? I had agreed not to tell Kallie about the votes because I didn't want her to be hurt. How could Marcus break that trust? He had hurt Kallie and betrayed me.

I looped Gozo's lead rope around a peg and ran into the tack room to get his saddle and bridle. But I wasn't fast enough. When I came out Marcus stood on the other side of Gozo, facing me. He leaned against the post with one hand on his hip.

"Tracy," he said, "I'm sorry about yesterday. I shouldn't have mentioned your name."

"Maybe you should be apologizing to Kallie," I said, "not to me."

Marcus shifted his weight. "I'm going back to L.A. Sunday," he said. "Tell Kallie good-bye from me."

At that moment, a dam broke inside me. Marcus was ducking out! He had shattered Kallie, and now he was leaving. And he didn't even have the guts to stay and apologize.

"Maybe it's good you're going!" I blurted with venom. "You never liked being here! You hurt Kallie on purpose! She's not an Oreo. She happens to be both African-American and white. There's nothing wrong with that! As a matter of fact, it's a great way to be. But mostly she's just a person.

She's my friend. And now she's avoiding me! You know what I think? I think that you don't have the guts to stay here and apologize, to admit you were wrong."

"I have to leave." He swept his arm towards the window, in the direction of the Montagues' big house. "They're making me leave!"

"I don't believe you! Why would they make you leave?"

"Do you really want to know, Tracy? Grant found drug paraphernalia in the field on Wednesday! Someone took a hundred bucks from his wallet! Guess who he's blaming."

"If you're telling the truth, if that even happened, why haven't I heard anything about it?" I demanded.

"Grant said to keep it private. He said that if I have a drug problem, it's my business. But I have to go home. He won't be responsible. Not even Andre knows. Not that it matters!" Marcus's voice was bitter with anger.

"Are you guilty, Marcus?" I asked.

"No, Tracy." Marcus looked down at the barn floor. "Maybe it was stupid for me to say what I did to Kallie. But I don't do drugs. I don't steal." For some unknown reason I knew Marcus was telling the truth. I knew it as surely as I knew the sun would rise in the morning, as completely as I knew my grandfather would die.

Marcus looked back up at me. His eyes fastened to mine. He said quietly and distinctly, "When you're black, you're born with a strike against you. Inside people's hearts you're guilty until proven innocent, stupid until you prove you're smart. You have to take what you can get when you can get it. That's what Kallie didn't understand. Maybe I should have told her that Grant Montague thinks I steal and do drugs because I'm black."

"No," I said. "Grant Montague isn't like that! Don't you understand that? This has nothing to do with your being black! It's just the circumstances. He doesn't know who else it could be. He's probably really worried about you! Maybe you should focus on that instead of feeling sorry for yourself because you're black!"

Marcus blew up. "I don't feel sorry for myself for being African-American! I'm proud of being African-American!" He shouted at me with his hands clenched into tight fists. I noticed the veins in his arms, the power in his muscles. I was suddenly afraid.

For a moment we stood there, facing each other. Marcus must have seen the fear in my eyes because he looked away from me and stroked Gozo's neck. "Tracy," he said in a voice that was both deep and musical, the voice Kallie had fallen in love with. "I'm not blaming you. You're a sweet white girl who doesn't know the score."

Marcus continued to gently stroke Gozo as silence spread around us. I grappled with my own feelings. I had been so angry at him. But I wasn't mad anymore. I knew he was like all of us, trying to find his way and falling all the time.

"You're leaving in two days," I finally said, "and you've never ridden these horses. I'm going riding. Want to come?"

"I don't know how to ride."

"I'll teach you," I said simply.

"OK," Marcus said.

As I went to get Capricorn's saddle, I wondered if I was doing the right thing. After what Marcus did, was I being too forgiving, too wimpy? Danika would have flattened him, and here I was about to teach him to stay on top of a horse.

I thought about Kallie. How would she feel? Then I realized I could always leave the cinch loose and watch Marcus flip upside down when he tried to mount, the saddle falling underneath the horse's belly. I laughed out loud. I knew I wouldn't do it. But it felt good knowing I could if I wanted to.

Chapter 20
SNAKES

"I'll never get used to this, Teach." Marcus gripped the horn while Capricorn loped.

"You're doin' good for a beginner, cowboy," I said with my fake western accent.

Marcus nearly bounced out of the saddle as he urged Capricorn into a trot. I couldn't help smiling. He looked stiff and proud as he flew up into the air each time the horse moved. "Can't we slow down now?" Marcus asked. I pulled Gozo down to a walk and Capricorn followed suit.

"You're from Michigan," Marcus commented as he continued to grip the saddle horn. I think he was trying to get his mind off of the fact that he was on top of a horse. He continued, "I've never been out of California. What's Michigan like?"

As I told Marcus about Michigan I found that he was a good listener. When I paused, he encouraged me to go on, so I described the colors of the fall, the beauty of the lakes, and the snow on the trees in the winter. "Then there comes a magical day after months of cold when you feel spring in the air," I explained. "You can actually smell it and almost taste it. But a few weeks later it storms and snows again. It's like Mother Nature purposely teased you. But when spring finally *does* come it's mega muddy. The summer is green and humid."

After I finished running on about Michigan, we rode for a while without talking. Marcus looked so uncomfortable on top of Capricorn. "Are you totally hating this?" I asked.

Marcus let out a short laugh. "Horses aren't my thing," he said. "But I'd like to see Michigan. I wonder if I'll ever get out of California. I want to get away."

"Travel to faraway places. Be all that you can be. Join the arrrmy," I sang.

"No thank you, ma'am," Marcus said. I laughed.

"Why did your family move here anyway?" Marcus asked a moment later. "If Michigan was so beautiful and all?"

"To be near my grandfather."

"Kallie told me that he's sick," Marcus said. "That's too bad." Then I found myself telling Marcus all about Grandpa and his cancer. It felt good talking to someone who wasn't emotionally involved, who just listened to me. But there was an edge of unreality about it too. I was confiding in Marcus, the guy who had broken my trust, who had hurt my best friend.

We rode for a few more minutes. Then Gozo became extremely agitated. He reared and shook his head violently. I kept my seat and dismounted as soon as I could. I looked at his nose. It was swollen and nearly double its normal size. I loosened the bridle strap and he settled down a bit.

"Marcus," I said. "I have to walk this horse back. Something's wrong!"

Back at the barn, Marcus watched while I carefully took off Gozo's bridle. "Something must have bitten him," I said as I examined his nose.

"Last week, Grant warned us to be careful in the fields," Marcus said. "The early rains have forced rattlers out of the ground." Marcus looked intently at Gozo and then at me. "If this swelling gets much worse he won't be able to breathe."

"I'll get Anita," I said. I shoved my hands into my pockets to keep them from shaking.

"Grant and Anita have gone golfing. The house is locked." Marcus's voice held an edge of bitterness. "I think Grant was afraid I'd take something. What's the vet's name? I'll call from my place."

It seemed like time froze while I waited for Marcus. I tried to get Gozo to drink from a bucket of water, but he tossed his head away. Then he stood very still. I think it was taking most of his energy to breathe. Over and over again I closed my eyes and silently prayed.

When Marcus returned, he was carrying two pieces of cut-up hose. "The vet said it sounds like a rattler bite. Gozo was probably snooping around and stuck his nose into a snake. We're supposed to insert these hose segments into his nostrils. I cut up the garden hose. Anyway, this will keep the airway open. If we can get these in, the vet said, Gozo can probably handle the snakebite."

Marcus held Gozo's head while I tried to force a hose piece into his right nostril. Gozo shook himself out of Marcus's grasp. I tightened the rope holding him. We tried again. Finally, I positioned the hose in his nostril. The next one was easier. Once in, the swelling held the hose segments tightly in place. Exhausted and frightened, I collapsed on a bale of hay and tried to catch my breath.

"Anytime you need help saving a horse's life, just ask me," Marcus said as he found a seat on another bale.

Marcus's voice calmed me. "Thanks, cowboy," I said. "I couldn't have done it without you."

"I'm a natural with horses," Marcus added.

"I could tell by the way you rode," I teased. Marcus laughed, and I found myself laughing too, laughing with tears in my eyes as the tension and terror left me.

"How can we laugh at a time like this?" I asked.

"Insanity!" Marcus shouted. The irony of it made him laugh even harder, and I realized that his laughter was a powerful weapon against fear and pain.

I went over and stroked Gozo. His strawberry roan coat was smooth and soft. I fondled his ears. He relaxed and his eyes closed as his breath whistled through the hose segments. "Marcus," I said, "why did you come to Haltsburg? What is it like in L.A.?"

It surprised me how easily Marcus opened up. Kallie had said he didn't talk much about himself, even with her. But this time was different. Maybe he figured he didn't have anything to lose since he was moving.

Marcus described the poor neighborhood his family lived in where his dad was the minister of a black church. He had five little sisters.

He told me about one fall day when he was about nine. He had stayed home from school to tend his sisters. His parents were at the hospital because his mom was in labor. A neighbor lady came over and told Marcus to go play for a while. She'd watch the babies.

Marcus took off. He rode his bike to a nice section of town where there was a huge wooden park that had been designed by children. It had wooden tepees painted yellow and red, huge wooden forts, a tree house slide, and a wooden merry-go-round—not the kind of merry-go-round with horses but the kind you push and jump on. It was very cool. That morning, there were only a few white preschoolers and their parents at the park.

After playing by himself for a while, Marcus noticed that some of the kids had climbed on the merry-go-round. He went over to push them. He ran as fast as he could, with the little kids screaming and laughing. The sun shone brightly overhead, the clouds whirling as Marcus ran. Then he leapt on. Somehow in the process, a blond boy about three years old fell off.

The child's father ran and picked up the crying boy and handed him to a woman. While the child screamed, the man yanked Marcus from the merry-go-round and pushed him down. "Why did you push my son off? Idiot! Why?" the man raged.

Marcus continued, "I ran to my bike and took off. I was crying so hard I couldn't see. I almost ran into a woman with a stroller. The guy kept yelling, 'You idiot! You stupid idiot!' I knew the man wouldn't have treated me like that if I were a white kid. When my parents brought the baby home that night, I told them what had happened. Dad told me to forgive. But all I could think about was how much I hated that white man."

"Some people are jerks," I said.

"But I keep wondering," Marcus said. "I keep wondering if I treated Kallie kind of like that white jerk treated me."

Marcus studied a piece of straw. Then he looked up at Gozo. He turned toward me. "There was another snake," Marcus said. His voice was almost a whisper. He went on. "I was locking up the church one night when this car pulled up next to me. A gang of white boys got out and pushed me into the trunk. They were drunk. They told me there was a poisonous snake in there with me.

"It was dark like a tomb. I felt the snake by my leg. Its scales were dry, not slimy. I grabbed it and twisted it until it went limp. When they let me out, they laughed at me. I had killed a harmless garden snake. Then they beat me up.

"But getting beat up wasn't the bad thing. The bad thing was being in the trunk and feeling so scared.

"After that I was filled with hate. That's why my dad sent me here. To learn to care about people who weren't members of my church or my family, to get to know Grant Montague, a good white man. To learn to forgive. I guess it didn't work." After Marcus said that, he stood up and walked out of the barn.

Tears stung my eyes. Why did people hurt other people like that? Growing up is hard enough when people are kind to you. How much harder it must be when you're mistreated.

Truth is knowledge of things as they were, as they are, and as they are to come. Some knowledge hurts. But it helps you to understand, too. Now I understood more about Marcus, and I cared about him.

Grant and Anita got home just before the vet arrived. Marcus disappeared while I ran out to the car and told them what had happened. A few minutes later, Dr. Runyon, the vet, pulled into the driveway. After checking Gozo, Dr. Runyon assured us the horse would be fine.

While Anita and Dr. Runyon talked about follow-up care, Grant walked me to my car. He wore tan shorts and a navy golf shirt. I thought about how good looking he was for a middle-aged guy, with his graying hair and steel gray eyes.

"Thank you, Tracy," Grant said. "You've got a good head on your shoulders."

"Marcus helped," I said. "A lot."

Grant nodded. Then I found myself blurting, "Marcus doesn't do drugs or steal from people. I know that."

Grant's gray eyes looked troubled. "Tracy," he said, "sometimes we don't know people as well as we think."

"It couldn't have been Marcus," I repeated as I studied the dust on my car.

"I wish you were right," Grant said, "but there's too much evidence. The pieces don't fit any other way. I'd let Marcus stay if he'd fess up and get some help. I even told him that I wouldn't tell his dad. But Marcus won't fess up. I've already called Theo. He's coming down tomorrow, and they're going back on Sunday."

I got into my car. "But how can he fess up to something he didn't do?" I asked as I shut the car door.

Chapter 21

THE NORTH STAR

It was six-thirty when I finally got home. Mom was in the garage folding laundry. "Hey, Mom," I greeted her as I got out of the car.

"There's pizza in the fridge." Mom handed me a stack of towels. "Put these away on your way in! Then unload the dishwasher and clean the kitchen!" She went back to folding.

"Sure, Mom, right away, on my way, this very day. I'll put these away, whatever you say," I saluted, as I took the towels.

"Thanks, hon," Mom said shortly, hardly looking at me. Did she even notice my sordid attempt at poetry? I wasn't just her slave daughter. I was a human being too.

For a moment, I felt this urge to stop and demand her attention. I wanted her to understand *my* life. But where would I start? It was so complex with events and relationships piled on top of each other, making a crazy web with no perceivable pattern.

I could begin by attempting to explain my relationship with Andre. Then I could tell her how Kallie had been hurt by Marcus, and how I had told Ms. Hahn about Dad. Then there was Marcus, who was innocent but presumed guilty by Grant. I would have to explain that. Not to mention Gozo's snakebite and the hose in his nose so he could breathe and sneeze with ease. And what about Brice? What would Mom say if I told her that I had absorbed his sense of humor in a futile attempt at sanity?

I glanced back at Mom. Her shoulders bowed under the weight of another load of laundry. She was tired too. I shrugged and went into the house.

After I divided the towels between the two bathrooms, I went into the kitchen and warmed up three pieces of sausage and pepperoni pizza in the microwave. Not my favorite, but it would do.

The telephone rang. I picked it up and said hello.

"Trace!" It was Kallie. The energy in her voice sounded forced, not real. "I tried to call an hour ago," she said. "Were you at the barn the whole time?"

"Yep. Gozo was bitten by a rattlesnake. He's OK though. We cut pieces of hose and inserted them into his nostrils to keep the airway open." I didn't tell Kallie who "we" was.

"You're kidding!" Kallie gasped. "You sure he's OK?"

"Yeah, the vet checked him. Is everything set for your baptism tomorrow?"

"Yep," Kallie said. "Elder Jarom was transferred so I asked your dad to baptize me. Sister Carlin's coming over in a few minutes. We're going to get something to eat and talk. Is your talk ready?"

"Just about."

"I better go," Kallie said. "Sister Carlin's supposed to be here any minute, and I'm not dressed."

"Kal," I said, "what are you doing tomorrow night? We could eat at Mammoth Burger and check out some videos."

"It's a date," Kallie said. I heard a doorbell in the background.

"It's Sister Carlin. I gotta jam."

"Bye, Kal." After we hung up the telephone, I headed for my room to work on my talk. Then I realized that I had left my scriptures at seminary. I went out in the living room to ask Grandpa if I could borrow his. He was hooked up to his oxygen and appeared to be resting. I didn't want to disturb him. I quietly took his scriptures. I knew he wouldn't mind.

The next day, as Kallie and my dad walked down the font stairs into the water, Brice, who was sitting in front of me, turned around. "This is so cool!" he whispered. He reached back and squeezed my hand. Brice actually looked nice today—so normal and missionaryish. I was glad he was there. After all, you can't have too many friends.

"Tracy and Brice sitting in a tree . . . ," Robbie whispered. I jabbed him with my elbow. Katie giggled.

I ignored them and focused on Kallie. She beamed up at me. Tears crowded my eyes. She looked so beautiful, with the baptismal clothing white against her dark skin and her hundred braids banded together at the nape of her neck. She was so strong, good, and brave. I was lucky to have her as a friend. "I love you, Kallie," I mouthed to her. But her eyes were already shut, waiting for the prayer.

Dad said the baptismal prayer and gently put Kallie under the water. She came up again with her ebony braids shiny and dripping. Sidney ran down the steps into the font, high heels and all. She embraced her soaking daughter. "Hallelujah!" she exclaimed with tears of joy. "I'm so happy you found the Lord!"

"Hallelujah, Mama," Kallie said softly.

"Sidney, we have more white clothes in the closet if you want a turn," Dad said, and everybody laughed. After Kallie had changed into dry clothes, it was my turn to talk about the Holy Ghost. It wasn't a long talk. I described how Jesus told his disciples about the Comforter. Then I explained how the Holy Spirit guides us and teaches us the truth.

"We need guidance today more than ever," I said. "I think of how the North Star guided the slaves to freedom and how the Liahona was a compass that led the Nephites through faith." I opened Grandpa's scriptures. I read part of two verses I had found the night before, flipping through his

Bible. The large print was bright yellow from Grandpa's highlighter. " 'For our gospel came not unto you in word only,' " I read, " 'but also in power, and in the Holy Ghost. . . . And ye became followers . . . of the Lord, having received the word in much affliction, with joy of the Holy Ghost.' "

I then told how the Holy Ghost would be Kallie's Liahona and her North Star. I bore my testimony and said how thankful I was to have the most important knowledge in the world—the knowledge of the truthfulness of the restored gospel through the gift of the Holy Ghost.

After I finished my talk, I sat back down. Brice turned around and gave me a thumbs-up. Did I really believe the things I said? Did I really have that kind of faith in the Holy Ghost?

Then the room became quiet while Dad, with the bishop and missionaries assisting, confirmed Kallie. While they administered the gift of the Holy Ghost, I heard sniffling in front of me. I opened one eye and glimpsed a Brice wiping his eyes.

Later, at Mammoth Burger, Kallie laughed. "Your burger lost its guts. You don't have a big enough mouth!" I had just tried to take a bite of my Double Mammoth Burger. I ended up with hamburger bun in my mouth and catsup on my face. The insides of my Mammoth fell out the other end of the bun.

"It's a coordination problem," I said. "I can't open my mouth and hang onto a Mammoth Burger at the same time."

"Speaking of problems," Kallie said, "I'm over mine. No more PMS. I'm moving on to other men. How's ADD?"

"Better," I said honestly, realizing that I'd gone through almost an entire day hardly thinking about Andre.

"Back to Marcus," I said. "There's some stuff I need to tell you." Kallie sat very still as I told her everything. How Marcus had helped me with the horse, how we had talked and our friendship had deepened, how Grant was forcing him to leave. Kallie listened carefully to each word. She sat so still I couldn't tell whether or not she was crying inside. When I finished, the silence between us thickened, like a dark wall. Did she hate it that I had become friends with Marcus just when their relationship had dissolved? Had I, in caring about the guy who hurt her, damaged my friendship with Kallie forever?

I didn't have the quiet strength Kallie possessed. The tension between us crushed me. "Kal!" I said, splintering the wall of silence. "Please talk to me! I had to tell you what happened!"

Kallie spoke. Her voice was tight as she struggled to keep her emotions in check. "Trace, thank you for telling me. It's just hard for me to talk about Marcus. He knew where he could hurt me the most, and he plunged in the knife. He dissed my opinion. He dissed the person I am. On purpose. I don't know if I'll ever be able to get over that."

Kallie bit her lip and continued. "Right now, I'm trying really hard not to care if he goes home tomorrow, not to care if I ever see him again. But you're right. Marcus doesn't do drugs, and he's way too principled to take anyone's money."

A few minutes later, Kallie ordered two extra large Sabertoothed Fries and a couple of Chocolate Woolly Milkshakes to go.

"Come on, Trace," she said as I grabbed the food and followed her out the door. "Let's go get a couple of romantic comedies. It's all we have left."

We spent the evening in front of the tube at Kallie's house, stuffing ourselves. After all, we both agreed, food and fantasy were the only true cures for PMS and ADD.

Chapter 22

A Beautiful Morning to Die

When I got home that night, Mom met me at the door. There were tears in her eyes and a dishrag in her hands. I remembered another day long ago when she had met me at the door with a similar look in her eyes and a twisted rag between her fingers. It was the day my horse, Topie, had been sold. She hated telling me that I would never see him again.

"Grandpa's dead, isn't he?" I blurted, my insides wringing as I grappled with the gaping hole Grandpa's passing would leave in my universe.

"No," Mom said. "He's slipped into a coma. It's close now, sweetheart. Very, very close."

Mom dropped the dish towel and tried to hug me. But I pushed past her and ran to Grandpa's bed. I sat down on the chair next to him. I wanted to say good-bye. I *had* to say good-bye.

Grandpa's eyes were closed, and there was a weird rattling sound each time he took a breath. Recognition wrenched my heart. It was the death rattle. I had read about it in a novel. I knew the sound would ring forever in my ears. I hugged myself, sobbing.

Katie forced her little body through my sobs and into my lap. "It's OK, Tracy." She wrapped her arms around my huddled form. "Grandpa's going to be with Jesus soon."

"I don't *know* that!" I choked. "All I know is that he won't be here for me!"

Then Katie started crying too. "I want Grandpa," she wailed. "I want Grandpa!"

The confused, crescendoing agony of my baby sister's cries stunned me. My sobs withered. Then this huge shuddering tenderness welled up inside of me, this need to comfort her. I slipped one arm around Katie and stroked her hair. I laid my other hand on Grandpa's still fingers. "Grandpa will be with us forever," I whispered as my tears dampened the curls on the top of Katie's head. I rocked her. "He'll always be with us," I repeated over and over again.

I rocked Katie that way for a long time. I rocked her until her tears stopped and she fell asleep, heavy in my arms. Then Dad lifted her from my lap and carried her to bed.

I went into the kitchen and stared at a chicken-and-rice casserole that had been left uncovered on the counter. Mom came in and put a sheet of plastic wrap over it and slid it into the refrigerator.

"Sister Vanlint made it," Mom said. "I'll have to ask her for the recipe." I thought about all the times the past few months that Mom had been tired, all the casseroles we could have used. Now the casserole was here. The death casserole. The death rattle. It was here because it was the end. My eyes filled again.

Mom came and put her hand on my shoulder. "Daddy said something a few days ago when we were talking about funeral plans." I knew Mom was speaking about her Dad, not mine. She was talking about Grandpa. "He said to tell you that in the Jewish tradition the new day begins with sunset and nightfall. He wanted you to remember that only in the darkness can we see the stars. And the stars are the bigger picture. He loved you a lot, honey. He also asked if you would bear a quick testimony at his funeral. But it's up to you. We know that you had a hard time at the service for Sister Wong."

I cried harder. Every part of me ached to hear Grandpa's voice telling me those words. Mom pulled me into her arms and held me like I had held Katie.

Later, I took a long hot shower. I let the water soak over me and rinse my tears down the drain. When I got out, I heard loud music pumping from Robbie's room. It was dark music, maybe Pearl Jam or Alice In Chains, so different from the Beatles stuff Rob usually listened to. The lyrics were about a deep hole, a lost soul, and broken wings.

The music was really loud, but somewhere within it I thought I heard Robbie crying. I knocked on the door. Robbie yelled that he was busy and to leave him alone. I knew he was hurting terribly, but I didn't know how to help him any more than I knew how to relieve the wrenching ache inside of me.

I went into the living room. Dad was on the couch, correcting lab notebooks, and Mom sat on the chair next to Grandpa, reading her scriptures.

"Please wake me up if Grandpa dies tonight," I said.

Mom and Dad both looked at me, then looked at each other. Dad nodded.

"OK, honey," Mom said. "Try to get some rest now."

I went to bed. Hours passed before I fell into a dark, shadowy sleep. At four-thirty, I awoke to Dad gently patting my shoulder. I followed Dad into the living room. Mom was holding Grandpa's wrist, listening for a pulse. "He's stopped breathing," Mom said quietly, "but his heart will beat a little bit longer."

I couldn't stand there waiting for my grandpa's heart to

quit beating. I silently stood up and walked to the front door. I opened it and stared into the night. Soon the sun would burn away the dark.

"It's over now," I heard Dad say to Mom. I turned around and looked at them. Dad held Mom, with his chin resting on the top of her head. I looked back outside. "Good-bye, Grandpa," I whispered. You died during the silent time, before the birds sang, when the sky was its darkest and the stars were their brightest.

A few minutes later, Mom and Dad came out and stood on either side of me. We waited until the birds began singing. We watched the sun rise, spreading its fingers of golden light.

"It's a beautiful morning to die," Mom said as tears trickled down her cheeks. I put my arms around Mom's and Dad's waists, and they put their arms around me. We stood that way for a long time. I thought of the giant trees that Grandpa loved. The trees whose roots wrapped around each other, holding each other up.

CHAPTER 23

SOMETHING MORE

At eight-thirty that morning I heard a car pull into the driveway. I looked out the window and saw the van from the mortuary. It had arrived to take away Grandpa's body.

As I numbly walked down the hall, I peeked into Katie's room. She was still asleep. Her baby-soft features moved slightly with each breath. The rhythm of human life. I went into her room and touched her downy blond hair. I kissed her cheek. It was so warm and silky. Her eyelids fluttered. She threw an elbow at me, pulled her pillow close, and fell back asleep.

"Trace?" I heard Rob's voice at the doorway. He looked gangly and cockeyed in his pajamas with his hair sticking up. He rubbed his red eyes. "Did Grandpa die yet?" he asked.

I nodded. "At about five this morning," I said. "They're here to take his body. Do you want to go out there with me?" I motioned towards the living room.

Rob shook his head. "I'm going to go eat breakfast," he said flatly.

A moment later, I was standing in the living room watching Mom and Dad take out the catheter and gently dress Grandpa's still form. Two men from the mortuary stood back. They waited patiently and respectfully. I wondered if they would be as respectful with the body when we weren't around.

Then the sound of an engine once again broke the quiet morning. I walked across the room and looked between the slats of the blinds. I felt sick in the pit of my stomach when I saw Andre's truck. Shreds of memory tumbled into my consciousness.

"Oh, no," I moaned, burying my head in my hands. I thought of how Andre had offered to come over and spend some time with Grandpa while we went to church Sunday morning. Today *was* Sunday. How could I have forgotten to call him?

"Trace, what's up?" I felt Dad's hand on my shoulder. I looked up and saw the question in his eyes.

"It's Sunday morning," I whispered. My voice felt hollow and barely audible. "Andre offered to stay with Grandpa while we went to church. I forgot all about it. I forgot to call Andre last night. How could I have forgotten?"

Dad was quiet. Thoughts ran through my mind. I thought about the rattlesnake. I thought about my talk with Marcus and about Kallie's baptism. I thought about the death rattle and Grandpa's body so still and so near. I thought of little Katie, so alive with her heart beating and her body so warm and dear.

So much had happened since Thursday. I hadn't had time to think about Andre. But how could I have forgotten him when Grandpa was dying? He loved Grandpa! How could I have forgotten him? How could I?

"Tracer," Dad said gently. "Do you want me to talk to Andre?"

"No," I said wearily. "Just ask the mortician to wait a little longer. I need a few minutes."

I slipped out the front door, closing it behind me. I walked out to the Toyota. Andre was in the truck, staring at the mortuary van. I went to the passenger's side and climbed onto the bench seat. I closed the door behind me.

I gazed at his black jeans and gray T-shirt. His black hair was clean and combed. I thought of how I was wearing the navy sweats I'd slept in, how I didn't have makeup on, how I hadn't even combed my hair. Yet Andre had expected me to be dressed up, ready for church. He had expected Grandpa to be conscious. He had expected to say good-bye.

Andre didn't look at me. He held a newspaper article in his left hand. He wadded it up and threw it out the window into the bushes. "I guess I won't need this," he said tightly. I thought of how he and Grandpa were always sharing knowledge—newspaper articles, books, quotes. But that was gone now.

Tears stung my eyes, and I brushed them away. I touched Andre's shoulder. "He died a few hours ago," I said gently. "They're here to take his body. You can come in and see him if you want."

Andre focused on the steering wheel. "I don't want to see his body," he said jaggedly. "I want to talk to him. Why didn't you tell me that he was getting worse?"

I sought for words to explain. "Everything was mostly the same until last night," I said. "When I came home from Kallie's, Grandpa was in a coma. It happened so fast. Everything became a blur. I forgot to call you last night. I'm so sorry."

"You just forgot," Andre said slowly, stonily, each word falling like granite, etched in pain.

"I didn't get to say good-bye either," I said dully. I longed for this conversation to end. The accusation and hurt in Andre's dark eyes was crushing me. I started to cry.

Andre started the truck and peeled down the street. He drove fast and angrily. The tires screeched, and rubber burned into the pavement. I tried to grip the seat, but centrifugal force pushed me against the door as he wheeled around corners. The windows were down, and the wind blew my tears away.

Andre turned down Grenacre Lane. We passed his house. I saw Theo's Buick. I glimpsed Marcus standing by the barn, staring at the fields. Yesterday was a million years ago, it seemed.

Andre slowed the truck when we came to Grandpa's land. He drove into the empty field and stopped. He got out, slamming the door behind him. He came around and opened my door.

He swept his arm toward the charred foundation of the schoolhouse. "It's gone!" he yelled. "The schoolhouse is ashes. Bart's dead! Where is your God right now, Tracy? You know that newspaper article I had? It was so cool! It was about a nuclear reactor that had been retrofitted for cancer patients. They inject patients with this boron solution that accumulates in tumor cells. Then the reactor generates a neutron beam that destroys the cancer. I knew it probably couldn't help your grandpa, but I wanted to show him. I wanted to give him some hope! If God existed, he wouldn't have taken Bart away from me! He would have at least let me tell Bart good-bye!"

Andre's words hit me like stones. "But your way didn't work either!" I choked. "The doctors couldn't save him! He's gone anyway! He's just a corpse!" I started shaking violently. I bent forward with my head in my knees, my sobs choking me.

I must have looked so pathetic that something inside of Andre softened. "Tracy," he said as he climbed into the truck next to me. Then he wrapped his arms around me, holding me tightly. I looked up at him. He started crying too. "Tracy," he gasped, "I'm sorry. I'm sorry."

I wrapped my arms around him. We held each other like that for a long time. "I want to be wrong," he finally whispered brokenly. "I want Bart to be alive somewhere. In some other dimension. In some other world."

"I just want him *here* with me!"

Then Andre cupped my face between his hands and kissed me. It was the first time I had been kissed like that. I kissed him back, tasting his tears. I felt myself disappearing in his arms, letting my loss and hurt melt into his warmth.

I felt Andre's heart beat against mine. His hands moved over my back and shoulders, and his kiss deepened. He pulled my body closer.

Then I saw Grandpa in my mind's eye, watching us and loving us both. I knew that what we were doing was wrong. It wasn't the right place or the right time. We were both so vulnerable right now and hurting terribly. We had a great deal of growing and changing to do. We had so much to learn. The world was before us, and there was a great deal to gain and a great deal to lose.

"Andre," I said as I pulled out of his arms and moved into the driver's seat. "I can't. I can't make out like this. I can't."

Andre looked at me. He looked so lost, so confused. Tears crowded in my eyes for the millionth time. What was I doing? I loved him.

"It's because I'm not a Mormon, isn't it?" His words were a statement, not a question.

"No," I heard myself say. "It's because *I am*."

I am, Brice had said at the dance. And I had immediately thought of the Old Testament, the burning bush, the voice of God. I believed in God. I was committed to Him. Committed to living a certain way. I looked into Andre's eyes, and I saw hurt there. I started to cry again. I forced myself to focus on the steering wheel. "I lost Grandpa today," I said. "I don't want to lose you."

"Tracy, I'll always be your friend. I guess I just wanted there to be something more."

"There is something more," I whispered. But my whisper was so soft that Andre didn't hear.

Chapter 24

THE QUALITY OF SOULS

We didn't talk as we drove away in Andre's truck. When we neared his house I asked if he would mind stopping for a minute. "I just want to see Gozo," I explained, "and tell Marcus good-bye."

"What's going on with Kallie and Marcus anyway?" Andre asked as he pulled the truck into the driveway.

"They broke up," I said. I was trying to decide whether or not to tell Andre the entire story when Anita came out of the house and hurried toward us. The wind blew her soft beige blouse against her slender shape, and her dark flowing skirt twisted around her ankles. Andre and I climbed out of the truck and met her halfway up the long walkway. Anita's expressive mouth was twisted with concern.

"During sacrament meeting the bishop announced Bartholomew's passing," she said as she hugged me. "I came home right after the sacrament. Tracy, I'm so sorry for your loss."

Then she kissed Andre's cheeks the way people greet each other in Brazil. "Son," she said as she took both his hands in hers, "I knew you were looking forward to talking to Bartholomew this morning. I've been so worried about you!"

Andre hugged his mom. I noticed that they were about the same height with the same jet black hair and slender elegance. But Anita's skin was lighter than Andre's, and her eyes were the blue green of a summer lake—a contrast with Andre's dark eyes and smooth olive skin.

I left them there and slipped into the barn to see Gozo. He wasn't in the stall. Grant must have put him out to pasture. I went outside and whistled. This time I didn't have to climb the hill. He trotted to me with his tail flying high in the wind. He allowed me one quick hug before he cantered away. A few minutes later he was rolling in the mud.

I leaned against the fence and watched him. I was glad he was fine. Yet, it felt almost as if the last few days hadn't even happened. No snakebite. No conversation with Marcus. No baptism. But, it had happened. And now it was gone. Gone like my grandpa. Disappeared. A memory.

I heard someone behind me, and I turned around expecting to see Andre. But it was Grant who approached me. He had a beer in his hand, and his face was grim. He shouldn't have been drinking so early in the morning. He shouldn't have been drinking at all.

"Tracy," he said, "I'm sorry about your grandfather. We'll all miss him. He was my Sunday School teacher before I was drafted. In Nam, he wrote me every week, even after I stopped writing him."

I nodded. I didn't want to cry again. Grant sipped his drink and rested his booted foot on the lowest fence board. He continued, more to himself than to me, "You'd think messing up my own son would be enough. But, no, I didn't stop there. I ruined Theo's son too."

I didn't say anything.

"Marcus didn't take the money." Grant looked at me, and there was pain in his gray eyes. "Kevin. *My* son, Kevin, took it! He called yesterday and said he stopped by last Sunday when no one was home. He was broke so he lifted some cash from my wallet. He didn't bother to tell me. He didn't bother to ask. For all I know, he did the drugs as well."

I didn't know what to say. I knew Kevin had a drinking problem, but I didn't think he used anything hard.

"You know why Theo sent Marcus to me?" Grant went on. "He wanted his son to learn the lesson we learned in Nam—that comradeship isn't defined by the color of skin. And what did I do? I accused his innocent kid of stealing from me, of doing drugs."

"Did you tell Marcus you're sorry?" I asked quietly.

"I tried," Grant said. "He walked away."

"Then you did your best," I said.

"You're a good kid, Tracy Barton," Grant said. "You have your grandfather in you. He and Theo Smith are the best men I've ever known."

"You're a good man too," I said. "That's why Theo sent Marcus here in the first place." I couldn't believe I was talking to Grant Montague this way. Was it because Grandpa had died and I had lost my inhibitions? Because I felt like I had little else to lose?

Grant stared into the wind as he continued. "Theo saved me in Nam."

"Andre told me that," I remembered aloud.

"He didn't save me from enemy fire. He saved me from myself," Grant said softly. "We were attacked, and the jungle turned into blood. In the confusion, I shot one of our own men. I killed him. A kid named Tyler Abridgo. You and Andre did a rubbing of his name when you visited the Vietnam Veterans Memorial. Anyway, when I saw what I had done I tried to shoot myself. Theo tackled me. 'God loves you,' he yelled. I still can taste the blood and dirt. 'God loves you.' I lost my faith in Vietnam, Tracy, while Theo became closer to his God. It's not a reflection on our religions. It tells you the quality of his soul compared to the quality of mine. It was my son I should have questioned, not his."

I didn't know what to say. Grant took another sip and sighed. "It was a long time ago. I never included that story in the letters to your grandpa. But the past doesn't leave you alone. And now there's my stepson. Andre's a great kid. I don't have to tell you that. I wish he'd join the Church, like his mom. But I'm not much of an example." Grant sounded so discouraged and so tired.

I wanted to tell Grant that things could be different. He could get rid of the drink in his hand. He could come back to church. He could be an example to Andre and Kevin. It wasn't too late.

But I didn't say anything. How does a seventeen-year-old girl tell a forty-plus man what to do? And I knew it wasn't as simple as it seemed. There were things in Grant's life I didn't understand; just as there were things inside Marcus that I hadn't fathomed; just as there were things inside Kallie and Andre that were hidden from me. Grant would have to find his own answers.

Yet, as the wind tugged on my clothes and hair, I couldn't help wondering what Grandpa would tell Grant right now if he were here. Somehow I knew that Bartholomew Andrew would have known what to say. Or maybe he just would have hugged Grant and remembered when Grant was a teenager, no older than Andre.

Chapter 25

STARS

"I'll call you and tell you the funeral plans," I said as I climbed out of Andre's truck.

"Don't forget." Andre looked at me and smiled, but his smile didn't cover the sadness in his eyes. He was missing Grandpa again. We both were.

"I won't forget. Not in a million years," I said as I closed the door.

Walking into my house, I heard chatter in the kitchen and looked in. Kallie and Brice were at the kitchen table, dressed in their church clothes. They were playing Rook with Rob and Katie. It was like a party. Katie gloated as she counted her points. She had just won a hand.

This didn't surprise me. Grandpa taught her how to play when she was five. Katie was adept at bluffing during bidding wars, raising the stakes, organizing trump, and getting the most out of the kitty. But just the thought of the game was a stone inside me. Grandpa would never play Rook with me again.

"Hey, Emerald Eyes!" Brice noticed me standing there.

"Trace!" Kal jumped up and hugged me. She wore her red dress, and she looked beautiful.

"Aren't you guys supposed to be in Sunday School or something?" I asked.

"When we heard about your grandpa we came to cheer you up. But now you'll need to cheer us up. Katie beat us bad!" Brice waved a white Kleenex in surrender. Then he got out of his chair and hung his arm around me. "Besides, I'd rather be with a beautiful breathless babe than sitting still in Sunday School."

I smiled. I knew I looked anything but beautiful and breathless with my sweats on and my face red and mottled from a morning of crying. But still, it was nice of Brice to say so. I was glad he and Kallie cared enough to come over.

"Brice and Tracy sitting in a tree," Katie chanted.

"Shut up, Kates," I said, remembering Andre.

"Yeah, Katie, I was talking about *you*, not Tracy," Brice teased.

Kallie looked at me carefully. "Trace, you look beat," she said as she squeezed my hand. "We won't stay long."

"Stay for lunch," I said. "We have all this food in the kitchen."

As we left the room, I tripped over the metal strip between the linoleum and the carpet. Kallie reached out to grab me, but it was too late. I fell flat. I sat on my duff, looking up at everybody, dizzy from exhaustion.

Robbie shook his head. "Trace, it takes real talent to trip over something that you've stepped over a thousand times."

"Are you OK?" Kallie asked as she reached down and grabbed my hand.

"It's DBD," I said. "Disintegrating Brain Disorder."

"At least it's not ADD or PMS," Kallie said as she pulled me up.

"I need to talk to you about ADD," I said. "There are some complications."

Brice interrupted us as he forced himself between us and put his arm around us both. "Tracy has ADD and PMS? Maybe I can be of assistance!"

"This isn't what it seems," I said. "Just code talk."

"Fill me in!" Brice said.

"Believe me, Bricey," Kallie sighed, "you don't want to know."

Brice and Kallie left about a half hour later. At that time, Mom was talking on the telephone, and Dad was snoring in his easy chair. I felt light-headed from lack of sleep. I needed to lie down before I fell down. I went into my room and crawled into bed.

When I woke up, it was dusk. I found Mom and Dad in the kitchen, writing down plans for the funeral.

"When's it going to be?" I asked, putting my arm around Mom's shoulder.

"Wednesday at ten," Dad said. "Casey can't fly in until Tuesday night."

"Tracy," Mom said, "I need to get the program printed. Have you decided whether or not you are going to bear your testimony?"

"I'm going to," I said, but I felt sick inside. Two years before, I had tried to speak at my seminary teacher's funeral, but I had blown it big time. Yet, if Grandpa wanted me to speak at his funeral I had to try.

A few minutes later I called Andre.

"The funeral is on Wednesday at ten," I said.

"I'll be there. Have you written your essay?"

"What essay?" My mind was totally blank.

"The one that's due tomorrow in Hahn's class. The interpretation of that poem by Sylvia Plath."

I really did have disintegrating brain disorder. "I completely forgot about it," I moaned.

"Hahn will understand if you turn it in late. But she won't let me off the hook," Andre said. "I can't understand the stupid poem. I'll have to bluff my way through."

"Good luck," I said. "Hahn calls all bluffs."

After we hung up I dug the poem out of my backpack.

Maybe working on it would get my mind off of Grandpa and Andre.

I read through the poem over and over again, but it didn't make any sense. Distracted, I gazed out my window. It was already dark outside. I stared at the streetlight, shining bright in the center, soft and filtered around the edges. It stood alone, and it dimmed the light from the stars.

I thought about Andre and his thirst for knowledge. I thought about our relationship. Did it have a prayer? I thought about the newspaper article Andre threw into the bushes—an article full of hope and knowledge. All the knowledge in the world hadn't been able to save Grandpa. But our prayers hadn't saved him either.

"Stop!" I told myself. "Stop thinking like this!" I jumped up and went out of my room. Robbie's light was on. I went into his room without knocking. He was sitting on his bed, with earphones on. He took them off.

"Want to go for a drive?" I asked.

"Where to?"

"Grandpa's land."

"OK." Rob grabbed his telescope and a flashlight.

When we got to Grandpa's land, I turned off the car lights. In the dark countryside, Robbie and I looked into the sky rather than at it. The night sky looked three-dimensional. We could tell that some stars were close and some very far away. They didn't just twinkle. It was as if they vibrated and pulsated, each with its own rhythm, its own song. I felt as if I were part of the sky.

Robbie set up his telescope. He pointed out Polaris and showed me different sections of the Milky Way. Then he named the constellations.

I remembered what Grandpa had said, that only in the darkness can we see the stars. And the stars are the bigger picture. I looked at Rob's dark skinny form, his lithe back forming a C as he looked through his telescope.

I thought about Robbie. He was kind of like Andre. He loved learning about black holes and parallel universes. But he was like Brice too—skinny, with a bizarre sense of humor. And he was just himself—a Beatles fan who dreamed of being a great basketball player but would never be tall enough. Still, when he grew out of his dweeby stage, there was every possibility he would be a neat guy.

"Robbie," I said, "do you remember when Grandpa took us to McDonald's and you barfed?"

"Yeah, the entire restaurant emptied in ten seconds. Grandpa laughed about it for a year."

"He laughed about it for the rest of his life," I added.

"Trace, do you remember when Katie told Grandpa she was going to do an experiment? She wanted to put some dirt and a watermelon seed under her tongue and see if they would grow there."

I grinned in the darkness. We had a very strange little sister. "Yeah," I said. "Grandpa told her to wait until she lost her front teeth because the seeds couldn't grow without sunshine."

We both laughed. Then I noticed that Robbie was in short sleeves. "Cold?" I asked.

"Freezing," Robbie answered. It was time to go home.

At home in my room I noticed Grandpa's scriptures on my desk. I had left them there after Kallie's baptism. I opened them and began reading everything highlighted in yellow, every scripture Grandpa loved most. It took me over two hours.

When I finished, I closed Grandpa's scriptures and stared at the AP poem that had been under them on the desk. I looked at the stars once more. Then I read the poem. Suddenly it made sense. I stayed up most of the night writing the essay.

Chapter 26

POSSIBILITIES

The next morning was cool and windy. I slept through seminary. When I got to school, I wondered if Andre would be waiting at my locker like in the olden days. But he wasn't. Then, during first period, Toni had her hands all over him. I decided that I was *not* going to stare at Andre and Toni like a jealous idiot. I knew that Andre had feelings for me. But I also knew I couldn't be physically intimate with him, not like Toni. Andre would have to decide what he wanted.

Ms. Hahn showed a forty-five-minute video about imagery while she graded our essays with a flashlight. In the darkened room, I saw Toni turn Andre's head toward her and kiss him. I still couldn't stand it. I cradled my head on my desk and closed my eyes.

"Earth to Tracy." Joan Lend, the girl next to me, elbowed me as the lights went on. I realized I'd slept through most of the video. Hopefully, Hahn hadn't noticed.

"Most of your essays need to be rewritten," Ms. Hahn said as she passed back our papers. Our essays were graded on a scale of one to five. If you got lower than a three you had to rewrite. So far that year no one had received a five.

"One essay was excellent," Ms. Hahn said when she had one paper left in her hands. My face turned hot. She hadn't returned my paper. She was talking about *my* essay.

"This essay is an example of the reader personally interacting with the poet's work. That process makes literature timeless." I stared straight ahead, not daring to look around as Ms. Hahn read aloud my essay:

" 'The title of this poem is "Words." Each image refers back to the power of words, to what they can do and what they are like. But the poem has another dimension. It is about life and death. That's where its strength lies, its timeless strength. After all, words are our vehicle for communicating; they lead us through life and beyond death.

" 'Words and life itself are like axes, and we are the wood. Pain strikes, and we ring with agony. And the echoes of our pain travel from the center of our souls like the beat of horses hooves, pounding the ground, pounding inside of us, hurting us over and over again.

" 'The sap from the wood wells like tears, like loneliness. We also cry and try to heal. Words are like water bringing life and hope. And in the water's mirror we find our own reflection as we search to establish meaning on this earth, this hard rock of human existence.

" 'Then death comes, the white skull eaten by weedy greens. The words are dry and riderless, for he who spoke them is gone. The human struggle is over. Is it meaningless? What is left behind? There are the indefatigable hoof taps, the voices from the dust, the words written down, the memories of those who still live.

" 'But is there anything else? Is there hope? In the bottom of the pool we find the fixed stars that governed the dead one's life. What are these stars? These stars extend into the depths of the pool and reach as high as eternity. They are for the living and the dead.

" 'But what are they? Perhaps one is a man's faith in God; perhaps another is the desire to learn and grow each day; perhaps another is courage; perhaps the brightest is love. My grandfather passed away this morning. These are the stars that governed his life. What are the stars that govern yours? What are the stars that govern mine?' "

The room was very quiet when Ms. Hahn finished reading. "Thus the power of words," she said as she handed me the essay. There was a big five written at the top.

Ms. Hahn sat down on her stool. "People," she said, "I've taught you about romanticism, collectivism, individualism, and existentialism. I'm teaching you everything I know.

"To me, the fixed stars in the bottom of the pool symbolize fate. The fact that our lives are governed by a cold universe of physical laws.

"I think about death a lot. In case you haven't noticed, I always tell you how old authors were when they died." A few people in the class laughed. We had noticed.

Ms. Hahn continued, gradually opening her arms with each statement until they were wide. "I also have a fixation for bats. I watch horror movies. I celebrate Halloween. I think it's important to laugh at what we're afraid of." Then she folded her arms, and her voice became low. "But deep inside of me, in that world of silent fear, I wonder how old I'll be when I die. I wonder how old you will be. When I read this essay, I saw the world a little differently. I didn't feel myself so much an insignificant part of a chaotic universe. I saw the possibility of comfort and faith. I saw the possibility of God. Thank you, Tracy, for that gift."

The bell rang. My face was beet red, and there were tears in my eyes. I hurried from the classroom as fast as I could.

At lunch that day, I saw Andre across the quad talking intently to Toni. Then Marcus came up and said hi to Kallie and me. Kallie was very cool. She didn't return his smile or maintain eye contact.

Marcus turned to me, "I'm sorry about your grandfather."

"Thanks," I said. "I'm glad things worked out with Grant. I'm glad you're staying."

"I am too." Marcus tipped his baseball cap and said good-bye.

Kal turned to me after he left. "Trace, if you want to wait for me after rehearsal we could go to Mammoth Burger for a snack."

"Sure," I said. "I'm feeling like a Woolly Milkshake right now." Kallie turned away and went to her next class without mentioning Marcus.

After sixth period, I ducked into the bathroom. Toni was in front of the glass redoing her makeup for rehearsal. Our eyes met in the mirror, and she wheeled around. Her eyes were red.

"Barton, I bet you're having a good day. A perfect ten. Hahn read your essay aloud. How am I supposed to compete with that? Then Andre broke up with me. You must be feeling pretty high right now!"

I stared at Toni. "Toni," I said, "I didn't know Andre broke up with you. I'm sorry."

Was I really sorry, or was I lying? I had never liked Toni Harris. I didn't consider her a valuable person with real feelings. Toni dropped her mascara into her purse. She whirled away from me and gripped the sides of the sink.

"The thing that really burns me is that I finally had something," she said, fighting tears. "I found a guy who was a really good person. I could talk to him, and he wasn't a sex fiend trying to get all he could from me. Then he tells me he isn't being fair. He really cares for you, even though you just want him for a friend. I couldn't believe it. You won. But you don't even appreciate it! It makes me sick! I love him!"

By this time, Toni was really crying. I was sorry. Sorry she was hurt. Sorry she couldn't understand, and sorry I couldn't explain. I knew how it felt. I touched her shoulder briefly before slipping out of the restroom.

After school, I waited outside the auditorium for Kallie to

finish with rehearsal. I sat on the grass and worked on calculus. I heard Ms. Hahn yell at the cast.

"You people have lost your rhythm! Stop thinking about your personal lives! Do you understand how important this play is? *The Winter's Tale* is about Leontes's obsessive, arrogant jealousy that destroys lives! Does that happen today? Yes!

"In the play, no one is left unscarred. Then time takes over and incredible possibilities become real. Tremendous possibilities exist if people have the courage, imagination, and energy to see them. You people have courage, imagination, and energy!

"This play is about the possibility of forgiveness. Think about this! Forgiveness!! Let the characters interact with each other. Let them hate, fight, and love! Let them forgive!!!"

I slipped into the back of the auditorium. I watched Andre, Kallie, Marcus, and Toni as they practiced the final scene in the play. In this scene, Leontes, the king, finds out that the queen, Hermione, is still alive. Hermione forgives Leontes for the anguish his jealousy caused years ago. I saw the passion and hurt in Toni as her eyes filled with tears when she looked into Andre's eyes. I watched Andre as Leontes the king begging her forgiveness. After the scene ended, Hahn and Rice clapped.

Chapter 27

THE REST ARE DETAILS

The next day after school, Andre and I went riding. I did figure eights in the field, showing off the things Gozo had mastered the past two months.

"Look at those lead changes!" Andre yelled from on top of Paulo.

I grinned and called back, "He's finally growing up!"

"I'll race you to the stream!" Andre urged Paulo into a gallop.

"Cheater!" I yelled after him.

Gozo wanted to take off, but I made him wait. It was important that he listen to me rather than to instinct. It was more important than winning. A few seconds passed, and I gave him the signal to run. We flew. My heart pounded as Gozo and I cut through the wind.

We gained some ground, but Paulo's size and head start made it impossible for us to catch up completely. When we arrived at the stream, Andre and Paulo were already there.

"I won!" Andre teased.

"Because you cheated!" I panted.

Andre grinned at me, and I smiled back into his eyes. I felt the electricity between us. Was there any future in it? What would time do to our relationship?

To escape my thoughts, I reined Gozo to the left and

started down a trail that followed the stream. The trail cut through a grove of eucalyptus trees. I loved their sharp smell and papery bark. I loved hearing the ripple of the stream and feeling the movement of my mount beneath me. I shivered in the brisk November air. This was being alive. This was joy. But even as I felt wrapped in the joy of life, a shuddering ache welled up inside me as sharp as the scent of the trees and as tender as the creek song. I wished there were no death in the world.

Andre pulled up alongside me. "When does Casey's flight come in?" he asked.

"Dad went to get her two hours ago. She's probably home right now. She said she's bringing a surprise."

"An engagement ring?" Andre suggested.

"Maybe," I said.

We rode a while longer in silence. "Are you thinking about Bart?" Andre finally asked.

"Yes," I answered. "And the funeral. I guess they go hand in hand."

"Do you know what you are going to say?"

I nodded, "I just don't know if I can get through it."

"You will," Andre said. "You're stronger than you used to be."

We were quiet for a little while. Then Andre's voice joined the sound of the creek and the wind. "I've made a decision. My grandparents in Brazil have been wanting me to visit for a long time. After Christmas, I'm flying down. I'm going to stay until college starts in the fall."

I didn't want to lose Andre, not when I had just found him again, not when Grandpa was gone. "Why don't you wait until after graduation? You can't leave your AP classes."

"If I go after Christmas I can enroll in a private Brazilian school. I'll take classes through the winter and summer. I'll really find out what it's like there. I've already been accepted at Stanford for next fall. I don't *need* the AP courses."

"Why?" I asked, trying to keep the tears out of my voice. "Why are you going?"

Andre focused on Paulo's mane. "Grant doesn't want me to go. He thinks I'm going through some kind of altruistic stage. But it's more than that.

"Last time I was in Brazil, I didn't want to be there. My dad took me there because he wanted me to learn to love Brazil, like he did. When he was shot, I vowed never to go back. But I keep having these nightmares. I'm in Brazil and I'm on a bus with a poor woman holding a smiling baby. I tell her how cute he is, and she takes the blankets off, and his feet are rotting. He's dying. The people on the bus all start crying and shouting at me. Then I wake up, but it's like I can still hear people crying. Marcus told me he's glad he left home. I just have to go."

We were quiet for a while. "I'll miss you," I finally said. "I hope you find what you're looking for."

"I'll miss you too." Andre studied me with those dark eyes. "But while I'm there I'll take your dare. I'll read the Book of Mormon."

"It's about time," I said, trying to lighten things up.

Andre smiled. "How did we ever get to be such good friends?"

"I don't know," I said, forcing myself to smile back at him. "Especially since my heroes are prophets and Apostles and your heroes are biochemists and physicists."

"It was your grandpa," Andre said quietly. "He's a hero to us both."

When I got home, Casey was waiting at the front door with her surprise. Her "surprise" was a six-foot-two guy with short platinum hair, baby-blue eyes, and little red circles in the center of his cheeks. Cupid in person! Chet from Idaho. The kind of guy you either loved or hated.

"So, this means you two are getting serious," I said as I surveyed them.

"Trace, we're engaged!" Casey flashed her hand which sported a pretty little diamond. I screamed and hugged her.

"I'm going to choke you both for not telling me!" I exclaimed a moment later. But even as I hugged Chet I felt this tugging loneliness inside. I had lost Grandpa. Would I lose Casey now too?

As the evening progressed, the wind blew harder and the temperature dropped. Mom warmed up Sister Jonsen's lasagna. Tomorrow, after the funeral luncheon, the food would stop. But the loneliness wouldn't. Would it go on and on until it was replaced by forgetfulness?

After dinner, Mom cheerfully suggested that Dad build a fire in the fireplace, the first one of the winter season. Rob brought in some logs, and Katie insisted on lighting the match. Soon the blaze warmed us all.

Casey and Chet went to the piano. Chet played while Casey practiced singing her song for the funeral. She had decided on "The Test" by Janice Kapp Perry. As we listened, Mom mentioned that Grandpa would have liked Chet. I agreed.

A little while later the doorbell rang. I opened the door and found Kallie and Brice grinning at me. Brice was holding a pot that contained an exquisite miniature bonsai tree. He handed it to me.

"How did you guys know I would love this?" I asked.

"Andre said that you and your grandpa had this thing about trees," Kallie explained. "He and Marcus helped pay for it. We all wanted you to know we're thinking about you. We love you."

"Thank you," I choked. I handed Kallie the tree and grabbed a Kleenex. "I'm such a boob. How will I get through my talk tomorrow?"

"Just look down at me. I'll be doing this," Brice said as he made this really stupid fish face. Suddenly, I was laughing through my tears.

Katie pushed her way in front of me.

"Come on in, guys," she yelled. "We're going to play Truth or Dare with Casey and Chet!" My little sister pulled Brice and Kallie into the family room. I didn't follow. Instead, I ducked into my room and put my beautiful potted tree on my dresser next to the amaryllis bulb Grandpa had given me after the fire. I walked back into the living room just as Chet chose "truth."

"So, Chet," Robbie said, "how did you *really* feel when you found out Casey has a grossly deformed baby toe?"

"I didn't know she had a deformed toe," Chet said innocently as he smiled at Casey.

"It's just a tiny bit twisted!" Casey threw a sofa pillow at Robbie.

Chet looked a trifle worried. I don't know if it was because of Casey's toe or if he was concerned about having Rob for a brother-in-law.

"Want to help me make popcorn?" I whispered to Kallie. "I'm not up to this game tonight." I couldn't stop thinking about Andre.

Kallie followed me into the kitchen. "Kal, truth or dare," I said as I put the popcorn in the microwave.

"Truth," Kallie said.

"Have you forgiven Marcus? You said he helped pay for the bonsai tree."

"I talked to him after rehearsal today. I don't think I've completely forgiven him, but we're on speaking terms."

"I'm glad," I said.

For a moment, we listened to the buttery chaos in the microwave. "I have a dare for you," Kallie said. "I dare you to write Brice on his mission."

"I plan on it. Kal, we're going to have so much fun rooming together at Ricks next year, then transferring to BYU."

"Absolutely!" Kallie said. "Unless ADD gets you first."

"I'm not getting married until I have my master's degree

in English and I've become Mizz Hahn the second," I cackled like a witch.

Kallie busted up.

"Besides, Kal," I said, "there are hundreds of Chets in Idaho and Utah. PMS and ADD might become ancient history!"

At the funeral, the sun shone through the chapel's stained glass windows. As Casey sang her song, I thought about my bonsai tree. I thought about how Grandpa took me to the redwood forest, how he taught me the names of the trees.

I looked at Kallie in the congregation, sitting with her family. I remembered her baptism and Sidney's hallelujahs. I glanced at Brice. He made a fish face at me. I smiled. Sister Miller, his mom, sat next to him as if a metal rod ran from the top of her head to her tailbone. She was as stern as Brice was mellow, as unforgiving as Brice was sweet.

I watched my family. Calm tears glistened on Mom's cheeks. Dad blew his nose loudly and pushed his glasses up. Rob and Katie were concentrating on something on the bench. I think they were thumb wrestling. Ms. Hahn sat on the other side of Dad. Mr. Littlejon was next to her. Before the funeral, Mr. Littlejon had told Dad that he would keep his advanced classes.

Finally, I looked at the bench that held Marcus, Grant, Anita, and Andre. Andre looked down at his hands. I couldn't look at him for very long. It would be my turn soon, and I had to gather my strength. I had a message for him—a message from Grandpa.

Casey sat down, and I stood up and started talking. "My Grandpa had two loves. He loved learning and he loved the gospel. He used to quote Albert Einstein, 'I am not interested in this or that phenomenon. I want to know God's thoughts; the rest are details.'

"Grandpa taught us so many things. He taught me about flowers and trees, how they live and grow. He taught my brother and my friend Andre about the stars. He encouraged us to read and talk and read some more. For as long as he could, he read my AP English books with me. He loved Shakespeare. He was fascinated with science. He and Andre threw ideas back and forth. They surfed the Internet and looked through the newspaper for interesting articles on research and medicine.

"I used to be angry at earthly knowledge, at the whole field of medicine and science. I felt like they let Grandpa down. They couldn't save his life. But Grandpa's faith didn't spare him from death either. It seemed like both of the things he spent his life learning about failed him in the end.

"But now I know that's not true. Two years ago, Grandpa had a heart attack. I was with him that day. Doctors did bypass surgery and saved his life. Earthly knowledge gave us two more years with him, and that was a wonderful gift.

"Grandpa's faith didn't let him down either. He told me once that scientific knowledge helps us answer the 'how' questions. That's what Einstein worked on. He wanted to know how God created this world. Bartholomew Andrew thought a lot about the other question: 'Why did God create this world?'

"And he found the answer in these words: 'This is my work and my glory, to bring to pass the immortality and eternal life of man.'

"I have a miniature bonsai tree in my room now. My friends gave it to me yesterday. When I look at it, I think of one of Grandpa's other favorite scriptures, from Isaiah sixty-one. It's a scripture about the gifts of the Savior. Now my grandfather is with my grandmother. He has beauty for ashes, the oil of joy for mourning; he is a tree of righteousness, and we are the planting of the Lord. Through him, and because of Jesus, God is glorified.

"When I looked at the stars last night, I thought about the stars that guided Grandpa's life, the fixed stars of courage, faith, and love. I could almost see my grandpa sitting with Heavenly Father and Jesus, but watching me at the same time. Through the whisper of the wind I know what he would have said to me and to you, 'Find God's thoughts through study and faith! For, like my friend Einstein said, the rest are details.'"

I looked down at a glowing Kallie, a solemn Marcus, and a winking Brice. I looked at Andre, and his eyes were wet. In my friends' eyes I felt the love of my grandfather, the same love Heavenly Father has for all of us. A love that is as deep as the night sky and as multidimensional as the universe.

About the Author

Marcie Gallacher received her bachelor's degree in education and speech therapy from Brigham Young University. As a credentialed teacher and tutor, she enjoys working with students of all ages. Marcie has served in many leadership and teaching positions in the Primary, Young Women, and Relief Society organizations. Her publication credits include an article in the *Ensign* and stories and poetry in *The New Era* and *The Friend*. She is the author of another novel about Tracy Barton, *Amaryllis Lilies,* which was published in March of 1997. Marcie lives in Elk Grove, California, with her husband, Gray, and their four children, Jamie, Matthew, Brett, and Michelle.